Thud! My tube hit something, and I turned around to see Ethan's blurred face. He was pressed up against the glass of his fallen goop tube, trying to get my attention. He pointed toward the main control room, where several Omegas were scrambling toward the rear door. The sign above the door said Escape Pod. Not all that comforting.

I looked back at Ethan, who had rolled over toward an instrument panel at the back of the room. His face, barely visible through the mass of yellow slime, was clearly panicked. I soon realized why—a huge monitor on the panel was flashing *Emergency* with a little timer underneath counting down the seconds.

23 . . . 22 . . . 21 . . . 20 . . .

It suddenly occurred to me: *Either these Omegas throw one crazy New Year's party, or I have twenty seconds to live. . . .*

mindwarp ™

Alien Terror
Alien Blood
Alien Scream
Second Sight
Shape-shifter
Aftershock
Flash Forward
Face the Fear
Out of Time

Available from MINSTREL® Paperbacks

mindwarp ™

Out of Time

by

Chris Archer

A
MINSTREL®
BOOK

Published by POCKET BOOKS
New York   London   Toronto   Sydney   Tokyo   Singapore

This book is a work of fiction. Names, characters, places, and incidents are either products of the author's imagination or are used fictitiously. Any resemblance to actual events or locales or persons, living or dead, is entirely coincidental.

A MINSTREL PAPERBACK *Original*

A Minstrel Book published by
POCKET BOOKS, a division of Simon & Schuster Inc.
1230 Avenue of the Americas, New York, NY 10020

mindwarp™ is a trademark of Daniel Weiss Associates, Inc.
Produced by 17th Street Productions, a division of
Daniel Weiss Associates, Inc., New York

ISBN: 0-671-02169-9

First Minstrel Books printing December 1998

10 9 8 7 6 5 4 3 2 1

A MINSTREL BOOK and colophon are registered trademarks of Simon & Schuster Inc.

Printed in the U.S.A.

To Richard, Margaret, and Hilary

Chapter 1

Todd

My name is Todd Aldridge. I was abducted on my thirteenth birthday.

Looking back on it, I suppose it's partly my own fault. I should never have snuck out of my house that night. In fact, my best friend, Bentley Ellerbee, had even warned me against it, but I'd ignored him as usual. That was the difference between Bentley and me. He was perfectly happy to sit home and watch people do exciting things on TV. Me, I wanted to experience it all for myself.

At least, I used to *think* I did.

A week earlier we'd both heard the same rumor, about how some trucker had seen a strange light hovering in the sky over the town reservoir. But while Bentley automatically assumed that the guy had seen a UFO, I needed to collect some hard evidence, to do a little investigating on my own.

If you knew me, you'd understand. I'm always reading mystery books or studying the wanted posters hanging in the post office. It's been my dream to be in the FBI for, like, forever. And even though you have to be twenty-one before you can even apply to the police academy in Madison, that night I figured I'd get an eight-year head start on some detective work.

Besides, I needed an excuse to test out the new birthday gift my stepdad had just given me: an X-1000 camera with special surveillance features, like a supertelephoto lens, autofocus, and an infrared filter for night photography. I knew that last one would come in handy since there were no lights around the reservoir. It was just this big circular lake, maybe a half mile across, in the middle of the woods that ran between the junior high school and the shopping mall. Mr. Holland, our science teacher, told us it was formed when a giant meteor crashed into Earth millions of years ago.

Whatever. There's a lot of talk about meteors around here. Part of it has to do with the town's name, which a lot of the time people think *is* Meteor because it kind of sounds that way when you say it. But it's actually spelled *M-e-t-i-e-r*.

As far as I was concerned, it might as well have been spelled *D-u-l-l-s-v-i-l-l-e*.

Honestly. *Nothing* exciting ever happened in Metier, Wisconsin. I knew this for a fact. The year before, for my twelfth birthday, my stepdad got me a police scanner so I could monitor the local crime reports and radio dispatches. In twelve whole months the most horrendous "crime" was when old

Ed Beister, Metier's resident nutcase, was found taking a bath in the fountain outside the municipal building. Not exactly an action-packed episode of *Cops*.

But all that's about to change, I kept telling myself as I made my way down to the water's edge. I mean, just think: If I could take a photo of the UFO, I might be able to prove once and for all that aliens did exist. Or else expose a hoax. Either way, I'd be sure to attract the attention of some secret *X-Files* branch of the FBI.

But—after about twenty minutes of crouching in the dark, in the weeds and the mud, getting eaten alive by mosquitoes—my grin had begun to fade. After *another* twenty minutes I almost wished that old man Beister would come along to take another bath. At least that way I'd have something to photograph.

I was about to pack it in when my camera started acting weird.

It began making a strange buzzing noise, vibrating in my hands as if it was possessed. Then its flash started going off nonstop, like a strobe light. It was acting so crazy that at first I didn't even notice how the clouds above me had started to glow and swirl together as something big and bright descended from above them.

My heart leaped into my throat.

I aimed my camera up at the sky. Peered anxiously through the viewfinder. Prepared to snap the prizewinning shot that would launch my career.

Then there was a blinding flash of light, brighter than anything I'd ever seen.

And everything went black.

I don't know how long I was out, but when I came to, it felt as if I was waking up from the longest nap of my life.

What happened to me?

My entire body felt weird—a mixture of aching and numb. There was a strange ringing in my ears and a horrible, bitter taste in my mouth. I tried to open my eyes, but the lids felt heavy, as if they were glued shut.

Had I been drugged? Kidnapped? Abducted by aliens?

As my mind cleared, I realized with a start that I was being carried—by at least two people. Someone held my wrists, and someone else had me by the ankles. Like any good detective, I decided to pretend I was still unconscious until I could learn a little about who was carrying me.

My first deduction was that whoever they were, they couldn't be too tall or too strong because they seemed to be struggling to lift me. Every couple of yards my rear end scraped painfully against the ground.

Gradually, as the ringing in my ears died down, I began to hear bits and pieces of a conversation. It faded in and out like a fuzzy radio broadcast.

". . . rest awhile? . . . arms are killing me . . ."

". . . not much farther now. Another fifteen minutes . . ."

It was two male voices. They sounded young—around my age—and *familiar.* Did they belong to someone I knew? I strained to hear more.

". . . can't believe he's still out cold . . ."

". . . won't be if you keep dragging him like that . . ."

". . . not *my* fault Todd's so heavy . . ."

My heart skipped a beat. Whoever it was knew my name! Maybe I didn't know *them*, but they sure knew *me.*

". . . in that tank too long? . . . do if he *never* wakes up? . . ."

". . . worry too much. I'm sure he's—*whoa!*"

The hands holding my ankles fumbled, nearly losing hold, then recovered.

". . . your step there . . . slippery . . ."

". . . where? I don't—*aaah!*"

Now the hands holding my wrists fumbled and *did* lose hold. I fell, my skull smacking the ground so hard that I saw stars. It was all I could do not to cry out. For a couple of seconds there was complete silence. Then:

"Yikes. We dropped him."

"Uh . . . do you think he's hurt?"

Great, I thought. *I've been kidnapped by Dumb and Dumber.*

"What do *you* think?" I said, sitting up, clutching

5

my throbbing head. I still didn't know who my captors were or where they were planning to take me, but wherever it was, I decided it would be safer if I walked there myself.

Once again there was a moment of stunned silence. Then:

"Todd! You're awake!"

"What was your first clue, Sherlock?" I muttered. I rubbed at my eyelids with my knuckles. No wonder they had felt heavy. They were caked shut with sticky goo. Wiping the crud away, I finally was able to blink open my eyes.

What I saw made me wish they were still covered with the crud.

The two figures bending over me looked like something out of *Night of the Living Dead*. Wide, bloodshot eyes stared at me out of filthy, blackened faces. Their clothes were ragged and equally dirty, as if the two of them had just dug themselves out of a grave—or climbed through a smokestack. One of them held a flaming torch in his hand that threw flickering shadows on our surroundings.

We were in some kind of underground tunnel. It was a big concrete tube, maybe six or eight feet in diameter. The air was cool and dank. Overhead, strange rootlike things hung down from wide cracks. They seemed to writhe like snakes in the firelight.

The zombie boy with the torch reached a hand toward me. "Don't be afraid," he told me.

"Too late," I answered, scurrying away backward like a frightened crab.

I got about three yards before I smacked into the legs of a zombie *girl*. "Todd!" she squealed.

I spun. This one was even more gruesome and freakish than the others. Her hair stuck out in every direction like Medusa's, and she had an extra pair of limbs growing out of her hips, like an insect.

"*Aaauuuugh!*" I hollered, my eyes bugging out of my head.

"Jack," Zombie Girl scolded once my scream stopped echoing. "*What* did you do to him?"

"Don't look at me," replied the boy with the torch. "He just freaked."

Hey. Wait a minute. . . .

"*Jack?*" I repeated, suddenly recognizing Torch Boy's voice. "Jack *Raynes?* Is that you?"

"Hey, Todd," he replied. "How's it hangin'?"

Jack Raynes was Metier Junior High's biggest clown. His game was trouble—particularly if it meant disrupting a class or a school assembly. My earliest memory of Jack was the time he convinced Sharon Flood to bring her trained mice in for show-and-tell on the same day that Cleveland Coopersmith brought in his one-eared Siamese cat, Fangster. (Let's just say that now there are a few less trained mice in the world.) "I should have known this was one of your practical jokes," I said angrily, rising to my feet. "'Let's scare Todd Aldridge on his birthday,'" I continued. "Ha, ha.

Real funny. The costumes are a nice touch, though."

"Costumes?" Jack said, looking all innocent.

"What do you mean?" said Zombie Girl, who I now recognized as Toni Douglas, one of our school's head cheerleaders. Now that my eyes had adjusted, I could see that her "extra pair" of legs actually belonged to a second girl who was concealed behind her. Toni was holding up the girl's legs; a third kid wearing strange, yellow rubber overalls supported the middle girl under the armpits. Together they lowered her to the ground.

"Wow," I said sarcastically. "This is quite an elaborate prank you all tried to pull off."

"This isn't a joke, Todd," Toni responded.

"*I'll* say," I cut in loudly. "Kidnapping is a federal offense." I twirled around accusingly. "I bet your dad would be interested to hear the things you're up to, wouldn't he, *Ethan?*"

I'd finally figured out who the other boy who'd been carrying me was. Even under his black makeup, Ethan Rogers looked like a walking Popsicle stick—nothing like his tall, muscular father, the chief of police for Metier Township.

"Todd," Ethan said in a low voice, "things must seem really strange to you right now, but we can explain everything. Honest. Just stay calm . . . *and please keep your voice down.*"

"*Why?*" I shouted at the top of my lungs. "*Afraid I might draw some unwanted attention?*"

"Todd, *please*," a girl's voice whispered frantically. It was the kid in the strange rubber suit. I glanced at her and was shocked to recognize Ashley Rose. She'd been in a lot of the same classes as me last year. I hadn't identified her at first since she wasn't dressed in her trademark outfit: black jeans, black turtleneck, and black army boots.

I frowned. Ashley had always been kind of a loner. It wasn't like her to play practical jokes or to hang out with other kids—*especially* kids like Jack. What was *she* doing here?

"Oh, forget it," Jack said, waving his torch at me in disgust. "If this is the thanks Todd gives us for saving his life, I say we just leave him. Let him fend for himself."

Saving my life? What were they talking about?

"Be reasonable, Jack," Ethan said, "Todd's obviously confused. He still thinks it's his thirteenth birthday."

"You mean it's *not?*" I said, suddenly alarmed. Just how long had I been unconscious? Days? Weeks? Longer? "Someone better tell me what's going on here," I demanded, trying to keep my voice steady.

Jack snorted. "You want the long version or the short version?"

"Whichever fits in the next two minutes," I said gruffly.

The others exchanged weary looks. Ethan sighed. "Okay," he began. "But first we need to ask

9

you some questions. Like, what's the last thing you remember before you woke up just now?"

"I was at the reservoir. It was around midnight. There was a strange light in the sky. Then you guys must've snuck up and knocked me uncon—"

"Yeah, yeah," Jack interrupted. "So what do you know about your father, Todd?"

The question threw me, but I decided to play along. "My stepdad? Um. He's a tall guy. Grayish hair. Does dad stuff—you know. Goes to work. Comes home. Calls me 'sport.'"

"Not your stepdad," Toni cut in. "Your *real* dad. The one who disappeared when you were four."

"Hey," I said, "how did you know that?" My father *had* walked out on our family when I was in preschool. But no one knew that except my mom and me.

"Because each of us also has parents who disappeared the very same year," Ethan explained. "My parents. Ashley and Toni's moms. Jack's dad. Elena Vargas's dad, too," he said, gesturing toward the girl who was lying near Toni and Ashley's feet, asleep. "They all vanished on the very same day . . . and they were all Alphas."

"All what?"

"Alphas," Ashley said. "Soldiers from the future. Part of a secret government project designed to create the ultimate armed forces. Humans, genetically enhanced to have special superpowers."

"Oh, of *course*," I said mockingly. "*Alphas*. And I suppose they use their superpowers to fight the big bad Betas."

"Actually, their enemies are called Omegas," Ethan said.

I started to laugh until I noticed Ethan's expression: dead serious.

"It was the Omegas who forced our parents to leave when we were little," Toni went on. "I suppose our parents figured that we'd be safer if they left. But we weren't. The Omegas wanted us kids, too."

"Why?"

"Because we have Alpha blood in our veins," Ashley answered. "And when we turned thirteen, we got Alpha powers."

This was getting interesting. "What sorts of powers?" I asked.

"Ethan has amazing fighting skills," Toni said, as if she had this routine memorized. "Ashley can stay underwater forever and swim like a dolphin. Elena can predict the future and astrally project herself. And Jack—"

"—is a master of communication," Jack interrupted. "I speak zillions of languages and can decipher all kinds of codes and foreign texts."

"What about you?" I asked Toni.

"I can store up electricity and release bursts of lightning through my palms," she told me, as simply as if she were saying, *I can crack my knuckles.*

11

"I'm also supposed to be able to jump through time," she added, "although I haven't quite figured that part out yet."

"Oh yeah, and we all have silver blood," Ethan added.

"Right, right," I said, trying not to show my skepticism. "I think I got it. You turn thirteen, your blood turns silver, you are issued a superhuman power, and then the Omegas come after you."

"Exactly, Todd!" Ashley blurted. "That's how it happens."

"Only in your case the Omegas got you *before* you changed," Ethan continued. "So your powers haven't had a chance to show up yet."

"The Omegas *got* me?"

"At the reservoir, Todd!" Toni exclaimed. "The UFO you saw was actually the Omegas' time machine. They abducted you and brought you back with them to the future. Then they placed you in a holding tank in their headquarters and kept you in suspended animation for months and months."

"Where you'd still be if we hadn't broken you out today," Jack put in.

"You're saying you guys rescued me?"

"You and Elena, who's still in suspended animation." Ashley pointed at the sleeping girl. "And then we blew up the Omega base, but they escaped in their time machine."

12

"Ah, I see," I said. "So . . . is that why you all look like zombies? From the, uh, explosion?"

"Yeah," Ethan said hesitantly. "You don't believe us, do you?"

I was silent for a moment, trying to digest everything they'd just told me. It was a lot to wrap my brain around. "I believe you," I said finally.

"You do?" Toni asked.

I nodded. "I believe you all are *completely out of your minds!*"

And with that, I turned and ran.

"Todd! Wait! Come back! Todd!"

The other kids' voices echoed after me. But I didn't listen. I just ran. It was hard to see in the dark tunnel. Impossible, actually. But that didn't stop me, either.

Sherlock Holmes had a saying about the impossible. Once you eliminate the impossible elements from a case, whatever remains, however unlikely, has to be your solution. I tried to follow his advice now, but when I eliminated all the impossible elements from what Ethan, Ashley, and the others had just told me, I wasn't left with anything. It was *all* impossible.

Alphas. Omegas. Silver blood. Superpowers. Suspended animation. Time-traveling UFOs.

Yeah, riiight.

I fell back on my original theory: This was all

just some elaborate practical joke. Those guys had hit me on the head, plain and simple, and then brought me down inside some sewer pipe. Why? I didn't care. The only thing I cared about was getting out of there.

I saw a dim light up ahead. I put on an extra burst of speed and soon found myself standing before a series of iron rungs set into the wall, leading up into a vertical shaft. The light was coming from above.

Behind me I could hear the other kids' rapid footsteps, getting closer. There wasn't any time to lose. Grabbing a rung, I started to climb. The metal felt cold and solid under my hands. *Finally*, I thought gratefully, *something real to hold on to*.

About twenty feet up I hit a heavy metal plate. It was some kind of a manhole cover or something. Bright sunlight filtered through several tiny, diamond-shaped holes. I pushed upward, throwing all my weight against it. With a stubborn groan it creaked open.

I wondered what I'd find above me. The mall? The school? I had no idea. Clearly I had a long way to go if I wanted to become a detective.

But even the best detective training couldn't have prepared me for what I saw next.

There was no mall. There was no school. There were only ruins, the devastated remains of a town.

A dry wind howled over the pockmarked terrain,

kicking up gray dust into a pale yellow sky. I had to cover my mouth and nose against the foul air. Concrete rubble, broken asphalt, and the crumbling skeletons of bombed-out buildings stretched as far as I could see.

I hauled myself out of the hole and looked around for anything that might tell me where I was. Was this some kind of government testing grounds, where they tried out new weapons? Even the sun looked different: It was too white and too harsh, like an angry eye in the sky.

I was beginning to suspect this wasn't a practical joke after all. Even Jack Raynes would have trouble changing the sun.

"Do you believe us *now?*" came Jack's voice from behind me.

I was too shocked to respond. I just stood there as the other kids climbed up next to me. Ethan helped Toni and Ashley raise Elena's sleeping form out of the hole.

Finally I found my voice. "Where are we?" I asked.

"Stranded," Ethan replied, "in Earth's far future."

"So it's all true?" I said. "About the Omegas, and them abducting me, and you blowing up their base and everything?"

In response Ethan pointed toward the horizon, where a thick column of black smoke was snaking its way into the sky. "That used to be the Omegas' dome."

Suddenly my legs felt weak. I sank down onto the dusty ground. "Wow," I said, hugging my knees to my chest. "I guess this means it isn't my birthday. Birth. Day. B-b-birth. D-d-d-day."

"Todd?" Ethan said, staring at me funny. "Is something wrong?"

I tried to answer him but couldn't. A strange sensation had taken over my body. My muscles were twitching under my skin. "Hap-p-p-p-p-p-pee bir-th-th-th-thday," I stuttered. I had no control over my mouth. It was as if someone else was using my tongue.

"Are you okay?" Ashley asked me.

"If you're going to barf," Toni added, crinkling her nose, "try to aim toward Jack."

"I-I-I'm f-f-f-feeling f-f-f-funny," I got out. My entire body was twitching by now. It was the oddest thing I'd ever felt, as if my skin was going to leap clean off my bones and slither away.

"What's he doing?" Jack whispered. "Is he going to faint?"

"No," Ethan replied, "I think he's about to find out what his power is."

Chapter 2

Toni

I stared at Todd, wishing there was something I could do. At first I had been like, *hello*, it's not even cold out, you can stop shivering now. But as his convulsions continued, I knew that something was really wrong.

He'd been the Omegas' prisoner for nearly a year, submerged in a tank. Maybe he'd gotten used to being in the tank's yellow liquid. Could he be suffocating now that he was out in the open air? He looked like a dying goldfish, the way he was flopping around. "Should I try to give him mouth-to-mouth?" I asked the others.

"Doesn't he look like he's suffering enough?" Jack replied.

"I'm *serious*," I persisted. "Maybe he needs oxygen."

But by then it was clear that Todd wasn't having a problem with his lungs. The boy was much more deeply disturbed. What had begun as shivering and twitching was now . . . well, *vibrating*. And it was totally off the Richter scale. His body was actually blurring, like the bristles of an electric toothbrush.

17

It was becoming hard to see his features clearly. First he looked like an out-of-focus movie, then like a big smear of Todd-colored paint.

As we watched in awe he slowly began to take shape again. I could just make out the outlines of his hands and legs. But they seemed different somehow. Bigger.

Then it was over, and Todd was sitting still again. Only he had changed.

Sure, he had the same black hair and the same blue eyes. But now he looked about forty years old.

"Is *that* his ability?" Ashley asked. "Superfast aging?"

"Cool," Jack said. "He can get a driver's license and go to R-rated movies!"

"I hope this doesn't happen each time his power engages," Ethan speculated. "By the end of the week he'd be the oldest man on the earth."

"Now *that* would be cool," Jack admitted. Jack had memorized the entire *Guinness Book of World Records*, which is, I suppose, the kind of thing you do if you're a thirteen-year-old boy with a lot of time on your hands.

"Shut up, you guys," Ashley said. "I think he's trying to say something."

The older Todd had turned in our direction. He wasn't really looking at us but sort of staring off into space. "Happy birthday, son," he said, smiling widely.

"Son?" Jack said, raising an eyebrow. "Who's he talking to?"

The older-looking Todd rose to his feet. More than just his size and age had changed. He was dressed in completely different clothes, too: a navy blue jumpsuit, the kind an astronaut might wear. I noticed a lowercase letter *a* stitched over the breast pocket in gold thread.

"If everything has gone according to plan," the older-looking Todd continued, "you should have just turned thirteen. Don't be alarmed at what's happening. What you're experiencing right now is just the manifestation of your special ability—a little biological birthday gift from your old man."

"Whoa," Ashley whispered. "That's not an older version of Todd. It's his *father.*"

"Could this get any *weirder?*" I whispered back.

"I can't hear your questions," the man went on pleasantly, "but I can give you answers, so just sit back and listen. You, Todd, are a kind of human recording device. And as a recording device, you're almost perfect. You have a photographic memory. You can store a limitless amount of information in your brain: text, pictures, video, audio, you name it." The man winked. "Homework is about to become a *lot* easier."

"Lucky stiff," Jack muttered.

"And that's not all," Todd's father continued. "You can do more than just store information. You

19

can also play it back. You'll discover you can perfectly mimic any sound or voice. Even holographic displays are no problem for you."

"What about video games?" Jack asked me under his breath. "Sega, Nintendo? Where do we stick the cartridge?"

Luckily Todd's dad couldn't hear. He just continued talking in his deep, friendly voice. "Right now you're playing back a three-dimensional image of me delivering this message. You can play back anything you've seen—all you have to do is look at it to scan it into your memory. This can be extremely useful. For example, by projecting someone else's image over yourself, as you're doing now, you can even seem to *become* that person. The perfect disguise."

I made a mental note that if we ever got back to the past, Todd was going to be my date for the prom. All he needed was a tuxedo . . . and Leonardo DiCaprio's face.

As I continued to fantasize about potential uses for Todd's skill, the holographic image of his father related the history of the Alphas and the Omegas. A lot of it we had already figured out.

Our parents, the Alphas, were the first batch of "supersoldiers" created by the U.S. government. Eight men and women who were genetically enhanced for survival in hostile climates and armed with superhuman powers. Unfortunately they had flaws. The military wanted cold, brutal killing machines who would follow orders blindly. But the Alphas were too human, too freethinking . . . and too *humane*.

The Omegas were the second batch. They were designed to be shape-shifters, with the power to change their form to look like anybody and the ability to survive in any climate, even in a postapocalyptic world.

With the Omegas, the government finally succeeded in removing the humane element from the human. Unfortunately they succeeded *too* well. The Omegas turned out to be so coldhearted, so *in*human, that they turned against their creators. Knowing they were devised to survive a nuclear holocaust, the Omegas infiltrated the Pentagon and launched a full-scale nuclear war. Humankind as we know it was destroyed, and the Omegas took over the earth.

Luckily the Alphas also survived. When they realized what the Omegas had done, they decided it was up to them to fix things. Alpha-1, also known as Henley, came up with a plan.

His idea was to time-travel into the past, find the scientist whose experiments with genetic engineering had led to the creation of the Omegas, and then convince him to abandon his research for the good of mankind.

Henley's plan seemed like a good one . . . with

one major downside. The same technology that would someday be used to create the Omegas had *also* been used to create the Alphas. If this technology were destroyed, the Omegas would be destroyed . . . *but so would the Alphas.*

In other words, it was a suicide mission.

Still, the Alphas knew it was Earth's only hope, the only way to be sure that the Omegas would never come into being. So they decided to make the sacrifice for the good of humankind.

They made the time jump into the past, landing in Metier, Wisconsin, of the 1980s.

But then one of them chickened out—Alpha-8, the only Alpha who knew the identity of the scientist—and the only Alpha with time-jumping powers. He vanished, stranding the other seven Alphas in the past.

With no means of going after Alpha-8 and not knowing where to find the scientist, the remaining Alphas had no choice but to wait it out, hoping that their eighth member might have a change of heart and return to get them.

It would prove to be a long wait.

In the meantime they lived the lives of normal humans. They got jobs. Bought homes. Settled down.

Henley and Alpha-6 got married and had a child named Ethan. The other Alphas married regular people in Metier and had children of their own.

And for a couple of years, at least, it was easy for them to forget that they were any different from anyone else. Living happy, simple lives in a small midwestern town, they could almost overlook the fact that silver blood flowed in their veins. They could almost convince themselves that the horrors they'd witnessed in the future were all just a bad dream.

Until the Omegas showed up.

"Somehow they had found us," Todd's father continued. "The Omegas knew that as long as we were alive, we were a threat to their existence. And as long as we posed a threat to *them, they* posed a threat to us—and our newly formed families. If the Omegas had found out we had you children, they would have come after you, too. So we decided to vanish, to fake our own deaths, to disappear without a trace. That way if the Omegas caught us, they wouldn't catch you as well."

But they did *find out about us,* I added silently. *They* did *come after us.*

Todd's father continued, his expression morose. "As persistent as the Omegas have been, though, I still worry that they will search for you. If they do, your only chance is to join forces with the other Alpha children. Find them, my son. Show them this recording. Make them your friends. Because together you must locate Alpha-8, the one who turned his back on us when we needed him the most. He alone knows the identity of the scientist who created us. You must get this information from him, find that scientist, and complete the Alphas' mission. The future of humankind depends on it. This is what Alpha-8 looked like when I knew him."

Todd's image blurred again. When he came back into focus, he looked like a thirty-year-old Asian man. He had close-cropped black hair and deep, penetrating black eyes. Although he stood only a few inches taller than me, I could tell that he was powerfully built. Bands of muscle rippled along his forearms, and cords of sinew stuck out in his neck.

"*That's* Alpha-8?" Jack protested. "Why, he could be anybody! Who knows where he could be?"

"I do," Ethan said, looking like he'd seen a ghost. "That's Danny Koto."

"Danny Koto?" Jack repeated.

"He teaches karate down at the mall," Ethan replied. "Well, *taught* karate. Back in the nineties. I took his class once."

"*That* part was easy enough," Ashley said. "We know who Alpha-8 is, and we know where to find him."

"Yeah," Jack replied. "Unfortunately *getting* to him will be another story. Look around. We're still stranded in the future."

"Only until Toni figures out how to use her time-jumping powers," Ashley said, looking at me encouragingly. I smiled uncomfortably.

"Like I said," Jack added, *"hopelessly* stranded."

"Oh, and I suppose *your* powers came with an instruction manual," I shot back. "'How to Be Annoying in Every Language.'"

Jack looked like he was about to respond, but Ethan cut him off with a wave of his hand, pointing back at Todd.

Our holographic friend was going fuzzy again. When the picture cleared, the image of Danny Koto was gone, replaced by that of an attractive African American woman in a similar navy blue jumpsuit.

There was a sudden tightening in my throat.

Mom.

"Hi, Antonia," she said, looking directly at me. "By now you have met Todd and know about the Alphas and our mission. As you will discover on your thirteenth birthday, you are what is called a jumper. As such, you have the ability to store and generate a massive electric charge. And it gets better, Antonia—you can focus your stored energy to create a hole in the very fabric of time and space. Then you can travel through that hole to any point in the past . . . or the future. You might have felt this power but are not entirely sure how to use it."

My mother raised her hand, and suddenly a tiny disk appeared in it. It looked like a miniature CD. "This data chip contains a detailed explanation on how to utilize your time-jumping skills—it's like an instruction manual for your powers."

Smiling smugly, I glanced over at Jack. His mouth had fallen open. "I don't believe it," he gasped.

My mother went on: "This is my gift to you, my daughter. But you must promise you'll be careful. Each time you jump, you could alter the history of the world through what we call the *ripple effect*. Say, for example, you jump back into the 1600s, and while there you step on and kill a butterfly. It's just an accident, the kind of mistake that happens every day. But what if that *particular* butterfly was supposed to be seen by a young man named William Shakespeare? And what if, after seeing it, he was going to be inspired to write a play? But now, because there's no butterfly, he never does. The whole world changes because you accidentally killed a butterfly."

Beside me Ashley let out a low whistle. "Bummer."

"And that's just the tip of the iceberg," my mother went on. "The farther you go into the past, the more violent and profound the changes can be. Make a mistake in the past, and the universe tries to readjust itself to heal the damage you've caused. These 'readjustments' multiply over time, getting bigger and bigger, turning into something called a *timequake*. It rips right through the space-time continuum, bringing enormous, tumultuous change in its wake."

I remembered the weird tremors that struck every time the Omegas launched their time travel

26

device. The fact that I could cause these tremors was a little scary.

My mother held up the tiny disk once again. "I'm going to pass all this information to you through Todd," she said. Then she seemed to hesitate. "I know you'll try to be good, Antonia. But you were always an impulsive little girl. I want you to promise me you'll only jump in an emergency, when you really have to."

"*I promise,*" I whispered.

My mother smiled. Had she heard me? "Good," she said. "Now take my hand."

The knowledge flooded into me like a stream of clear water. I could actually feel the information flowing out of my mother's palm—Todd's palm—and into my own. It felt alive somehow. *Fizzy.* Like a million tiny insects running up my arm, through my shoulder and neck, and settling in my brain.

It's hard to explain, but suddenly—just like that—I knew how to time-jump. It seemed almost second nature to me, as familiar as reading or riding a bike. Like I had been doing it all my life.

I shivered as I thought about all the places I could go: Forget Metier, Wisconsin—I could stand on the deck of the *Titanic!* Watch Cleopatra sail the Nile! Dance with Elvis back when he was thin and cute! But even though I was itching to try out my new skills, I remembered my mother's warning. I had to take this time-traveling stuff seriously.

I had sworn to use my power only when it was absolutely necessary. Besides, I couldn't just take off—my friends and I had a mission to accomplish. What had Todd's dad said? "The future of humankind depends on it." You couldn't really argue with that.

Still, a tiny voice said inside my head, *think of the possibilities.* . . .

I snapped out of it and looked around. I guess we'd been standing there longer than I'd realized. By now the sun had sunk well below the horizon and the sky was rapidly growing dark. A cold wind whipped around my bare legs, and I could smell the bitter tang of distant fires burning—the smoking remnants of the Omega base. I was hungry and my muscles ached, but I felt strangely supercharged. I was ready for action.

Todd, I was relieved to notice, was back in his own form. He and the others had gathered around Elena. The dark-haired girl was just beginning to stir. She moaned softly, then her eyes fluttered open. Raising her head, she looked around at us and smiled faintly. "Hey . . . guys," she said, her voice weak. "I knew you'd come . . . rescue me."

She tried to sit up, but the effort seemed too much for her.

"Take it easy, El," said Ashley, coming to her aid. "You're still feeling the effects of being in the Omegas' sleep tanks."

Once she was in a sitting position, Elena glanced around at the nightmarish landscape. Her brown eyes grew wide. "Where . . . are we?" she asked, her voice cracking.

"We're still in the future," Ethan replied.

Elena winced, raising a hand to her forehead as if in pain. "Rats," she muttered, sounding upset.

"No—don't worry about it," Jack responded cheerfully. "We have a way to get home now."

Elena shook her head. "You don't . . . understand," she said, rising unsteadily to her feet. "*Rats*," she repeated, more forcibly. "I see them . . . a whole swarm . . . closing in. . . . We have to . . . get away. . . ."

"What's she talking about?" Todd asked, looking confused.

That's right—Todd hadn't seen the rats yet.

"She's talking about *them*," Ashley said, pointing straight ahead. You didn't need Elena's psychic vision to see the dozens of tiny red eyes, glowing in the distance like tiny coals . . . and rushing our way.

"And *them*," I added, pointing the other way. Red pinpricks of light dotted the horizon in that direction, too.

"We're surrounded," Ethan stated. "Quick. Everybody back in the tunnel."

"Can't we just scare them off?" Todd asked.

He still didn't get it. "They're a little big for that," I responded.

"How big are we talking?" Todd asked nervously.

29

"You know how big a guinea pig is?" Jack said, crouching over the manhole cover.

Todd seemed to relax a little. "Sure," he said.

"That's about the size of one of their *paws*," Jack replied. "Uh, Ethan?"

"What?" Ethan answered.

"We got a little problem here. The lid is stuck."

"It's *what?*" Ethan came over and helped Jack tug on the round steel plate. It wouldn't budge.

"What do we do?" Ashley asked, a note of panic creeping into her voice.

The rats were getting closer. You could hear their claws, tearing across the rocky ground like a thousand sharp knives.

"I don't know," Jack said. He turned to me. "Toni. Use your powers or something. Time-jump us out of here."

"Why don't *you* use *your* power," I shot back, feeling defensive. "Speak rat at them. Tell them we're not tasty or something."

"Jack's right, Toni," Ethan said. "We can't outrun them and we can't outfight them. You're our only hope."

"I know, I know." I bit my lip. Suddenly I was nervous. What if my powers didn't work? Or if I didn't have enough energy? "I promised my mother that I'd only jump in the event of an emergency," I said, stalling for time.

By now the first rat was only ten yards away. It

advanced toward us slowly, its rodent teeth gnashing ravenously. In another instant it was flanked by two others. Then two more. As they moved toward us all five began hissing. The sound was wet and horrible, like the noise spit makes being sucked through your teeth.

"I'd say this is about as nine-one-one as it gets," Jack said.

"Okay, okay," I said. "Quickly. Everybody link hands. Form a circle."

We did.

I took a deep breath. Closed my eyes. Then I reached down deep inside myself and unleashed all the power I could muster in a swift, powerful flood. Energy exploded through my arms, through my friends' arms, round and round our six-person ring, faster and faster. There was a loud, low humming that steadily rose in pitch and intensity to a high, deafening keen.

With a hideous shriek the first rat leaped at us—
But we were already gone.

—— Chapter 3

Ethan

The instant we jumped, I was blinded by a brilliant white light inside my cranium. It was as if all my other senses had disappeared. I couldn't feel my body. Couldn't hear. Couldn't taste or smell. There was nothing but silence, and light, and lightness.

So this is what time travel feels like, I thought. *Amazing.*

The light was beginning to fade. I became aware of a low rumbling sound filling my ears. A couple of moments later I could once again feel Elena and Jack's hands, clutched tightly in my own, and then a hard surface materializing under my feet. Pavement.

The rumbling sound was getting louder. It seemed familiar somehow. Something in the very back of my mind was telling me that I ought to remember what the noise was.

And then, with a burst of pure terror, I did.

My vision cleared just in time to see the massive truck, honking frantically as it bore down on me and my friends. It was huge, an enormous black eighteen-wheeler. Its shiny chrome grill alone looked bigger than most cars.

We had landed in Metier all right, but we were in the middle of the street!

"Snap out of it!" I yelled to my companions. "We're about to become roadkill!"

I raced toward the curbside, yanking the others after me like a chain of human-sized paper dolls. We cleared the semi's path just in the nick of time. It roared past, followed closely by seven more eighteen-wheelers, all identical, like a convoy of ghost trucks. As they zoomed by they kicked up a stream of litter, which swirled around our legs in the diesel-smelling air.

For a full minute we just stood, panting, at the side of the four-lane road, catching our breath. Then we all broke out in whoops of joy.

"We made it!" Todd shouted, leaping in the air.

"We're back home!" Elena beamed.

"Nice landing, Toni," Ashley said. "Your directional control could use a little work, but other than that, I think you have the makings of a first-class time pilot."

Toni nodded wearily. The time jump must have really drained her. She looked as if she'd just run a hundred miles wearing a backpack full of rocks. "Jack, you can thank me anytime you like for saving your life," she panted. "Now, for instance."

"I'll thank you for saving my life," Jack said, "when I'm convinced it's actually safe. Right now, for all I know, you brought the rats with us."

"So, what do you think the date is?" Elena asked.

"Here's a clue," said Todd, bending to pick up a stray piece of newspaper lying by the curb. He peered at the date. "'June 27, 1998,'" he read, then scowled. "Aww, man. We lost a whole year!"

"Correction, Rip Van Winkel," Ashley told him. "*You* lost a whole year because you were asleep for most of it. *We* only left about a week ago."

"I've been gone for a year?" Todd asked, trying to adjust to reality. "My parents must be going crazy looking for me."

"I think more than your parents are looking for you," Ashley said. "Look." She pointed to a headline near the bottom of Todd's paper.

No Sign of Missing Teens
Four More Vanish, Total Hits Six
Police Suspect Foul Play

Next to the article were school photos of each of us.

"Ugh," said Toni. "I *hate* that picture."

"You know what?" Todd said suddenly. "I think I'll go home. I want to watch TV on my comfy couch and surprise my parents when they get—"

I shook my head sadly but firmly. "No, Todd," I told him. "You can't do that."

"What do you mean?" he demanded. "My mom gets frantic if I'm even a few minutes late coming home from school. I've got to let her know I'm okay."

34

"Think about it," I replied. "If our disappearance was such big news, our *reappearance* is going to be even bigger. Not only will we alert the Omegas to our location, but the police are going to want answers as to where we've been. Answers that will land us in a mental hospital."

"What you're saying," Todd said, "is that we can't blow our cover."

"Exactly," I replied. "From now on, we're undercover. I know you want to see your family. I want to see my parents, too. But not enough to risk their lives. Or mine. The mission has to come first."

"I guess I can live with that," Todd decided. "If I've been missing for a whole year, a few more days won't hurt."

"Let's get started," Jack said, turning to me. "Where do we find this Mr. Koto guy?"

"Well . . . that's going to be a little tricky," I replied.

"What do you mean?" Elena asked. "I thought you said you knew where he was."

"I guess I should have mentioned that Mr. Koto died last October. Even if that newspaper is recent, we're still eight months too late."

"Hey, no problem," Todd said. "Toni can just jump us back another year to when he was still alive."

We all looked at Toni. She was sitting on the curb, swaying back and forth, her eyelids drooping with exhaustion. Suddenly she realized we were all staring at her. "Oh no," she said. "Uh-uh. No way. No more time jumping today."

"But Toni," Ashley said, "we have to get there sooner or later."

"Please, Toni?" Elena pleaded.

"I say we take a vote," Todd added. "All in favor, say—"

"Leave her alone!" Jack cut in sharply. "Can't you see she's beat?"

Toni looked at him, surprised. "Gee, thanks, Jack," she said.

"I say we go to the mall and get some pizza first. Then we'll make the jump."

Toni snorted. "I should have guessed there was something in it for you."

"For me?" Jack asked, batting his eyelashes. "Whatever are you talking about? I just think that after the swell job you did getting us back to the twentieth century, we should celebrate with a triple-decker deluxe with extra pepperoni. Or two."

After two weeks of eating nothing but rat stew, the thought of pizza made my mouth water. Obviously the others felt the same way.

"I suppose Jack's right," Ashley said. "Toni needs to recharge before she uses her powers again. And we could all use some food."

"We definitely need to get cleaned up," I added, looking around at our soot-smeared faces. "We look like a bunch of coal miners."

36

"But is going to the mall such a smart idea?" Elena asked. "Everyone is looking for us. What if we run into someone we know?"

"Well, it's not the greatest idea. But I would kill for a pizza. If necessary, I'd even go on an SUPM," Jack said.

"A what?" Elena asked.

"A solo undercover pizza mission. I'd smuggle some out for my comrades, of course," Jack said, grinning widely.

Elena laughed. "All right. But we should try to stay off the main roads."

"No prob, Bob," Jack said. "I know a shortcut."

"Pizza is the perfect meal," Jack said as he guided us through the woods around the reservoir. "Every food group is represented. You have tomatoes from the vegetable group—"

"Tomatoes are fruits," Ashley corrected.

"Okay, brainiac, so they're from the *fruit* and vegetable group. The pizza dough is from the bread group. Cheese from the milk group. And if you get a Coke with it, that's something from the all-important carbonated beverages group."

"What about meat and fish?" I asked.

"Pepperoni and anchovies!" Jack replied. "Or if you prefer, barbecued chicken."

"Stop!" Toni moaned. "I'm getting too hungry to make it to the mall!"

"That's not all that's standing in your way," I told her. "Look."

We had just pushed our way through the tree line surrounding the rim of the reservoir. There, about thirty yards away, were the eight black trucks that had nearly run us down before. They were parked in a row along the gravel road that skirted the body of water.

"What do you think they're doing?" Ashley asked. She was whispering, and I didn't blame her. Something about the unmarked vehicles seemed . . . well, *ominous.*

Just then a group of six men rounded the side of one of the trucks. Or at least I think they were men. They were dressed in strange silver suits that covered their entire bodies, with built-in boots and gloves. Their faces were concealed beneath hoods with mirrored face shields, and they were carrying something in a crate. Something heavy, from the looks of it.

"It looks like they're wearing contamination gear," Todd told us. "But those aren't police. And they're not in the army, either."

We watched in silence as the men in silver pushed open the enormous door at the rear of the truck. It rose up like a garage door, revealing the cargo hold. With a coordinated effort they lifted the crate and shoved it inside. It must have weighed a ton. One of the men climbed up into the back of

38

the truck. He turned around, reaching up to close the door . . . and froze.

"Uh-oh," Toni muttered. "I think we've been spotted."

For a second the man just stood there, motionless. Then he pointed at us, saying something to the men on the ground. The others swung around to face us.

"What do we do now?" Ashley asked nervously.

"They're probably just some friendly maintenance workers," I suggested. "Let's try waving."

The six of us waved.

The friendly maintenance workers started charging toward us. "Let's try running," I said.

The men in the contamination suits barreled through the forest like dogs after an escaped convict. Maybe we could outrun them, but I wouldn't put money on it.

When I looked over at Toni, my hopes sank even further. She was gasping for breath, barely able to keep up. The time jump had been too much for her. "Guys!" I shouted to the others. "We can't run. Let's hide."

Moments later we were all crouched inside a sewer pipe, holding our breath as a group of the contamination men fanned out over the forest. If you're ever in a sewer pipe, I highly recommend holding your breath.

Just when I thought our luck might hold, one of the men pointed toward the pipe. Soon two of them were headed our way to investigate. We were trapped.

I felt a funny fluttering at my elbow and looked over to see Todd vibrating in place. His outline blurred, and he became a five-and-a-half-foot smudge.

"What's he doing?" Ashley whispered to me.

"I don't know," I replied.

Then Todd's features started to come back into focus. Except it wasn't Todd anymore—he looked just like one of our silver-suited pursuers! I instinctively backed off, remembering how many times we'd been duped by the shape-shifting Omegas. Then Todd's voice said, "Relax, guys. I'll take care of these morons."

He hopped out of the pipe and strolled easily up to the two men in contamination suits. After a brief exchange they turned and walked away. Todd headed back to us, already flickering back into his black-haired, blue-eyed, thirteen-year-old shape.

"What happened?" Toni asked. "What did you tell them?"

"I told them I'd already checked the pipe and there was no sign of those meddling kids any-where," Todd said proudly. "Now, who's for pizza?"

Chapter 4

Jack

I stared at the locked doors of the mall in horror. I couldn't believe the words in front of me. My worst nightmare had come true.

Closed for Remodeling
Please Excuse Any Inconvenience

"Inconvenience?" I shouted. *"Inconvenience?* I haven't had a slice of pizza in, like, two hundred years!"

Ashley came over and put a hand on my shoulder. "I guess we should have known. The last time we were here, the Omegas crashed their UFO into the food court," she reminded me. "What did you expect them to do—stick a Band-Aid over the giant hole in the ceiling?"

"So the place is a little messy," I protested. "Is that any reason to deprive a growing boy of the pizza he so richly deserves?"

Just then a guy who looked old enough to be in college, wearing a tank top shirt and faded jeans, emerged from the front entrance to the mall. He had massive arms and shoulders and a menacing look on his face. He was walking briskly toward us.

For no apparent reason his stern look changed into a big smile. "Ethan Rogers? Is that you?"

"Kenji?"

"You know this guy?" Todd asked.

"That's Kenji Koto," Ethan replied as the young man headed toward us across the parking lot. "Danny Koto's son. Good timing. He's one of the few people who can actually help us."

"What are you doing here, Kenji?" Todd asked as Kenji walked up to shake hands.

"Checking out my dad's old studio. It's a wreck. Very depressing. Do you mind if we get out of here?"

A few minutes later the six of us were piled in the back of Kenji's rusty blue pickup truck, pulling into the dirt driveway that led to the late karate master's house. I suppose you could call it a cabin, but the two-story building was unlike any cabin I'd ever seen. There was something strange about the way the logs and stones were put together, but I couldn't put my finger on it. "My father built this house himself," Kenji told us proudly as he parked the truck, "the same year that he adopted me."

Ethan shot me a look. I knew what he was thinking. *Adopted.* That explained why Kenji didn't have super Alpha powers like us.

We walked up the short flight of wooden stairs

into the house. Suddenly I realized what was so different about the building. "There aren't any nails or mortar," I remarked.

"That's right," Kenji replied. "My father built it according to ancient principles. All the pieces interlock by themselves. According to traditional beliefs, the house is stronger this way."

"Are those traditional Japanese beliefs?" Toni asked.

Kenji shook his head. "Navajo," he replied. "Dad was a real Indian nut. Have a seat—make yourselves at home. I'll be right back." He disappeared into the back room.

"What we're looking for is any kind of information that your dad might have left behind," Ethan called after him.

"Like what?" Kenji shouted from the other room.

"Anything at all," Ethan replied. "Letters, photos—"

"How 'bout this?" Kenji said, returning with a small, leather-bound book. "It's my father's journal. I found it after his death. Unfortunately I've never been able to translate it."

Translate? Could it be? Someone finally had a use for my special power? "Let me get a look at it," I said. "*I'll* translate it for you."

Kenji stared at me. "It's in ancient Japanese, I think," he replied. "But even the professor of Asian studies at my college couldn't make it out."

"No prob, Bob," I replied, motioning for the book with one outstretched hand.

43

Looking doubtful, Kenji passed the book to me.

Cracking it open, I stared at the elegant Japanese symbols, which I knew were called kanji. I focused in on the page, waiting for my power to kick in. After a full minute, I was still waiting.

"Uh, Mr. I-Can-Read-Anything," Toni said, nudging me, "you're holding it upside down."

Oops.

"Right," I said. "I know. I was just trying to, um, get all possible perspectives on it. Before I read it. To ensure total accuracy." Toni wasn't buying it. "Forget it," I told her, "it's a secret power thing. You wouldn't understand."

Turning the journal the right way around, I began to read out loud.

Mr. Koto's diary was written in a very tight, direct style. He didn't puff himself up, and he didn't apologize for his actions. For example, right on the first page he admitted that he was a coward and a traitor who had betrayed his friends, the other Alphas. I glanced up at Kenji at these words, expecting him to ask me to stop reading. But he didn't, so I continued.

As we had already learned, the government had engineered Akira "Danny" Koto to be a jumper, just like Toni. And they did a pretty good job. In fact, the team of scientists working on the project were so overjoyed at their success that they didn't realize the implications. You see, a jumper is the perfect escape artist. There's no jail on earth that can hold a time traveler who wants to get away. And once Mr. Koto realized what the government was up to—that he and the other Alphas were going to be used as weapons of war—he decided the best place for him was pretty much anywhere but there.

So it was Mr. Koto's powers that let the Alphas escape from the government lab where they were being kept as virtual prisoners. He freed all of our parents, risking his life as he did so.

Once they'd escaped, the Alphas figured they had foiled the government. What they hadn't known was that work had already begun on the Omega project. When the Omegas launched their insidious plot to take over the world, the other Alphas called upon their friend to help them once again.

They asked Mr. Koto to use his jumping skills to transport the Alphas back into the past, where they could convince the scientist who had created them to destroy his work. At first Mr. Koto agreed. He found out the identity of the scientist and would have told the others—

But then he had second thoughts.

He didn't want the Omegas to destroy the world—and yet he didn't want to commit suicide, either. So, rather than take the Alphas to the proper destination, he landed them in Metier, Wisconsin, in the 1980s. Then he abandoned them, jumping himself even farther into the past, to the 1930s.

Mr. Koto lived anonymously for many decades,

vowing never to use his powers again—for good or for evil. All he wanted to do was put his past behind him. But as he grew older and wiser, his conscience grew louder and louder. Finally he couldn't stand the guilt any longer. He returned to Metier as an old man, hoping to find out what had become of his former friends. That was in 1990.

But by then his fellow Alphas had already been captured.

Devastated by this discovery, Mr. Koto decided to stay in Metier. He built his house. Adopted Kenji. He even set up a studio to do what he did best, teach self-defense.

Then, seven years later, Ethan Rogers walked into his classroom. Mr. Koto instantly recognized the thirteen-year-old as the son of Alpha-1, Henley.

Mr. Koto saw an opportunity to correct the wrongs he'd done. He would give Henley's boy the one clue he needed to solve the puzzle and save the future. The missing piece that he himself had been too cowardly to reveal to the other Alphas all those years ago.

I stopped reading.

I had come to the bottom of the page. My hands were shaking as I turned over the thin piece of yellowed parchment. I was about to uncover the clue that would defeat the Omegas!

I held my breath, turned the page—and felt my heart sink.

The next page was blank.

A thin slip of paper marked the place where Mr. Koto had left off, never to write in his diary again. The bookmark fluttered to the floor like a dead moth.

I sighed heavily. "Great. I guess he died before he could write down the clue."

"Unless *this* is the clue," Ashley announced, picking up the slip of paper. She looked at it, then frowned. "Or maybe not," she added quickly.

"Why not?" Todd asked. "What does it say?"

"'Milk, prune juice, plums, toothpaste, toilet paper, Tums,'" Ashley read. "It's just a grocery list."

"Or the world's worst poem," Toni volunteered.

"There's more writing on the back," Elena pointed out.

Ashley flipped the paper over. We all peered over her shoulder. The writing on the other side was sloppy, as if it had been written down in a hurry.

MASON JL5.1945

"Do you think it's the clue?" Todd asked.

"It must be," Kenji said. "That's why the Omegas killed him. Somehow they knew he was about to reveal their secret."

"What—you think he was killed?" Ethan asked, startled.

"When my father died, he was one hundred

years old, but he was as healthy as a man half his age. They said he died in his sleep, but I never saw the body. And though I pleaded for it, there was no autopsy. Draw your own conclusions."

He said the words with such force that even I knew better than to argue.

"My father obviously wanted to right the wrongs he'd done in his life," Kenji continued. "He wanted to help you, the children of his friends. As his son, that obligation falls on me."

"Thank you," Ethan said. "But I think we can manage."

My stomach chose that moment to make a noise like a bear during mating season.

"Well," Ethan conceded, "maybe some of us could use something to eat."

"Right," Kenji replied, "and even though I don't have your superpowers, my nose tells me that some of you might want to use the showers in the back of the dojo."

An hour later we were beginning to feel a little more like the heroes we were supposed to be. Kenji had given us new clothing, food, and even some money. I was truly grateful, even if the food *had* been almost entirely healthy.

As we left the house Mr. Koto built we tried to figure out the meaning of the strange numbers. I was starting to be convinced that it was a clue after all. There were a few interesting possibilities that seemed to be worth looking into.

Maybe "Mason" was some guy's name and the rest was his birth date. The "JL5" could stand for July 5; the "1945," obviously, would be 1945.

Or maybe something happened on July 5, 1945, in a *town* called Mason. Or maybe the second part wasn't a date at all but a phone number. Or a locker combination. Or something else altogether.

Like I said, the possibilities were intriguing.

"We don't have any time to waste," Ethan said. "The Omegas will be coming for us. The sooner we figure this thing out, the better."

"We should split up into teams, like police detectives," Todd suggested. "That way each team can investigate a different angle and save time."

"Good idea," Ethan replied. "Let's get to it."

Chapter 5

Ashley

Somehow I got stuck doing the least interesting part of the mission: checking to see whether Mr. Koto's mysterious clue was a phone number. And to top it off, I wound up doing it with Jack.

"Are you sure this is the best way in?" I whispered.

It was a typical summer day in Metier, with temperatures in the high nineties. I'm sure that most kids were at swimming pools, splashing around and drinking sodas, or else catching the latest blockbuster down at the Cineplex. Instead of joining them, I was crawling on my stomach beneath the shrubs behind Jack's house.

"This is the only way we can be sure we won't be seen," he replied.

"Seen by whom?" I asked him. "I thought you said your mom and stepdad would be at work."

"Can you say *'Omegas'*?" Jack replied snidely. "Now, when I give the signal, cover me."

"Cover you with what?" I asked. "Dirt?"

Jack scurried off toward the house, then motioned

for me to follow. Keeping low to the ground, I joined him by the entrance to the cellar. I held open the tornado doors while Jack lowered himself into the darkness below. "Don't drop it on me," he warned.

"I've got it," I assured him.

Halfway down he stopped. "Hey, I've got an idea," he said, looking up at me brightly.

"What's that?"

"While you get the phone, why don't I check on my Nintendo? I'm worried that the Omegas might come for it and, uh, study it to figure out my fighting techniques."

Somehow the door slipped from my fingers.

There was a muffled *thud* and Jack said, "Ow! Okay, we'll play it your way. But if the Omegas learn the secret of my double penguin kick, it'll be on your conscience."

"I'll chance it," I told him.

Luckily there wasn't anybody home. Jack and I moved quickly and quietly through his house, like two characters out of *Mission: Impossible*. Five minutes later we were in the backyard, huddled in Jack's tree house and going over our loot.

We had taken only what Jack called "the bare necessities": a pitcher of lemonade, a box of strawberry frosted Pop-Tarts, two bags of potato chips, a stack of *Mad* magazines, a pen and some paper . . . and the cordless phone.

51

In one smooth, practiced move Jack tugged the phone's antenna out with his teeth, punched in a number with his thumb, then pressed the receiver to his ear. "We should be close enough to the house to have good reception," he informed me, digging in a bag of chips. "At least until the battery loses its charge." Suddenly his eyebrows shot up. "It's ringing," he announced.

"Wow," I replied, suddenly a little nervous. It occurred to me that we probably should have planned this out better. In the movies the heroes always know just what to do. What were we going to say to the person who answered?

"Well?" I asked after he'd been listening for a while. "Is anyone there?"

Jack cupped his hand over the mouthpiece. "It's a recording," he whispered through a mouthful of chips. "Someone who knows all about the Omegas and the Alphas." He listened some more, nodding gravely. "He says he has an important message, crucial to our success. . . . 'Whatever you do, you must listen to the kid who speaks all the languages.'"

"Give me that," I barked, snatching the phone from him.

The voice on the other end of the line had an important message, all right: *"This number is no longer in service. If you believe you've reached this message in error, please check the number and dial again."*

"Great," I said. "Dead end. We're out of luck."

"Not exactly," Jack shot back, reaching for the box of Pop-Tarts. "There are a couple hundred area codes in the continental United States, plus hundreds of international codes. I'd say our investigation has just begun."

I sighed deeply. It was going to be a long day. I just hoped my patience—and the Rayneses' phone bill—could take the strain.

———— Chapter 6

Ethan

Toni and I pushed through the dense brambles surrounding the reservoir. It seemed like the most sensible place to try our next time jump. No one would spot us there, and when we came through the other side—on July 5, 1945—there was less of a chance of being run over by trucks.

"Are you sure you can nail the exact date?" I asked Toni.

"I hope so," she replied, freeing her shorts from a pricker bush, "but I don't really know. Jumping isn't an exact science, like matching your shoes with your purse. I have to imagine our landing spot and try to hit it. It's like taking my best guess."

"You can do it," I told her, trying to sound reassuring.

Finally we found a clearing in what seemed like a good place to make our move. Toni took my hand. I braced myself, getting ready for the mind-warping lurch of time travel.

Then Toni hesitated. "Ethan?" she asked. "Why don't we just jump to the day before Mr. Koto's death? Then he can just *tell* us what his clue means and we don't have to deal with anymore running around."

I shook my head. I'd already thought of that. "Kenji seemed pretty sure that his dad was killed," I told her. "That means Mr. Koto was being watched before his death."

"Well, Kenji also seemed pretty sure that I was an extra large," she added, flapping her arms around ridiculously in the too big T-shirt she'd been given, "whereas I'm *clearly* a petite. Face it, his dad was a hundred years old! People have been known to just, you know, *die* when they reach that age."

"Still," I replied, "we can't chance it. If the Omegas were watching Danny Koto, they'd expect us to try to contact him. We've come too far to risk being exposed now. We have to go to the one place they're not looking for us—and that's 1945."

"All right," Toni answered. "But when we get there, you have to promise me something."

"What's that?" I asked.

"That you won't step on any butterflies."

The young boy stared at us, bug-eyed, his mouth hanging open in astonishment. He dropped what he was holding—a big rock of some kind—right on top of his foot, but it didn't seem to bother him. He was in shock.

I suppose I'd be in shock, too, if I'd just seen two

thirteen-year-olds materialize out of thin air. How were we going to tell this kid what had just happened? Fortunately he had an explanation ready for us.

"Are you Martians?" he gasped.

I looked at Toni. She looked at me. "Sure, we are," I said. "We're, uh, friendly teenage Martians."

"I knew it!" the boy said. "I *told* my friends there were Martians. But they didn't believe me."

"Well, you were very smart," Toni told the boy. "How did you figure it out?"

"Oh, I know all kinds of things," the boy said, kicking the dirt in front of him bashfully. "I'm going to be a geologist. See?"

He indicated a wagon resting behind him, a cherry red Flexible Flyer with the initials R. M. scratched into the paint on one side. It was packed high with rocks and clumps of dirt.

"What's in there?" I asked the boy conspiratorially.

"I probably shouldn't tell a Martian," he said, frowning. "But you seem okay. That's some new stuff for my rock collection. I've got geodes, volcanic glass, rose quartz, and . . ." He looked around to see if anyone was listening. "*Meteors.*"

"What's your name?" Toni asked him.

"Reginald," he said proudly. "But you can call me Reggie."

"Reggie," Toni asked, "how would you like to help your new Martian friends out by telling us today's date?"

"That's easy. It's July 5, 1945," he replied.

Bull's-eye! Toni smiled at me proudly. She'd done it.

"And what's *your* names?" Reggie asked us.

I couldn't resist. "My name's Luke Skywalker," I said, "and her name's—"

"Madonna," Toni chimed in.

Then, thanking Reggie for his help, we left him to his rock collecting and headed into town.

"Excuse me, I was wondering if you could help me?" I asked the prim, white-uniformed nurse behind the desk at Metier's Mercy Hospital.

"Yes?" she said. Her name tag read Dreedle, RN.

"I'm trying to find out if there have been any children born today named Mason."

"Born today?" she asked, and made a sour face.

"Well, since midnight of last night," I clarified.

"And are you a relative of this child?" she inquired.

"No, I'm a . . . friend of the family's," I said.

Nurse Dreedle studied me over her glasses. I flashed her my sickliest, goody-two-shoes smile, and she seemed to soften. "I'll see what I can do." She flipped open the admissions book. "You say the mother's last name is Mason?" she asked, going down the list.

"That's right," I told her.

Toni stepped over to the desk. "Although Mason

57

could also be the baby's first name," she said.

Nurse Dreedle glanced over at Toni. Her expression became sour again. "I'm sorry," she said, looking back at me. "Who is this?"

"She's a friend of the family's, too," I explained.

Nurse Dreedle looked at Toni, then looked at me, as if she were debating something. Then, sighing loudly, she rose from her chair. "Follow me," she replied.

"What's *her* problem?" Toni whispered to me as we walked down the hospital corridor. Nurse Dreedle was a good fifteen feet ahead of us—out of earshot, I hoped. "Did you see the way she looked at me? Like she hated me."

"That's ridiculous," I protested. "She was looking at both of us strangely, and I don't blame her. I mean, look at us. We're the only two people in 1945 wearing oversized T-shirts!"

"I suppose you're right," Toni said. She glanced down at her outfit with disgust. "I *hate* being underdressed."

By this time we'd reached the glass-fronted entrance to the obstetrics ward. There were only three babies in the window. Metier, after all, is a pretty small town.

"The little boy on the left was born today," Nurse Dreedle informed us.

"Is his last name Mason?" I asked hopefully.

She checked her clipboard.

58

"No," the nurse replied. "It's Beister. He hasn't been given a first name yet. His parents can't seem to decide between Rodney or Edwin."

Beister? I thought. *Ed Beister? Could it be?*

"I'll bet you a hundred dollars they pick Edwin," I said. *And that he likes to take baths in fountains,* I added silently.

Nurse Dreedle just stared at me. "I'm sorry. . . . *What* did you say your relationship with the parents was, exactly?"

"Well, *that* was fairly useless," Toni said as soon as we'd left Mercy Hospital.

The other two babies had both been girls. And neither one had the last name Mason. Or fathers named Mason. Or birthmarks shaped like mason jars, for that matter.

Now we were walking down Main Street—and attracting stares right and left. From the way people were looking at us, you'd think that they'd never seen a pair of Air Jordans before . . . and I suppose they hadn't.

Toni noticed the attention, too. "I think you were right," she told me as we crossed the intersection of Main and Van Buren. "It *is* because of the way we're dressed."

Main Street was still decorated with red, white, and blue banners from the Independence Day parade that had taken place the previous day. Here

59

and there the sidewalk was littered with confetti and streamers.

As far as I was concerned, the parade wasn't over. I was captivated by the diverse vehicles that cruised along the wide lanes beside us. It was like stepping into the pages of Dick Tracy or an old Superman comic. Everything from horse-drawn vending carts, to Model-T Fords, to newer models like Packards and Plymouths. ("Look at all the classic cars," Toni had remarked when we first saw them, before I pointed out to her that here in 1945, these cars were considered *modern*.)

"I mean, look around." Toni made a sweeping gesture. "All the men have crew cuts and are wearing hats, and every woman has long hair and a dress. . . ."

My attention was suddenly grabbed by a huge black Rolls-Royce heading toward us down the road. It was swerving wildly and showing no signs of braking.

Toni didn't notice. "Do you think we should do something about the way we look?" she went on. "Maybe go shopping for new clothes or someth—"

"Look out!" I yelled as the Rolls jumped the curb and sped onto the sidewalk right in front of us.

Without thinking, I grabbed Toni and dove with her out of the way as the massive car nearly mowed us down. Other pedestrians scattered like bowling pins as the Rolls barreled down the sidewalk, finally crashing into a lamppost.

The car door opened and the driver climbed out. He was a huge man, at least six feet tall, and easily three hundred pounds. His round, moon-shaped face was as pale as raw pizza dough and wore a blank, dazed expression.

Is it an Omega? I wondered, lying on the pavement next to Toni.

"What's the big idea, pal?" growled a tall man in a straw hat. "You nearly killed us!"

The driver didn't answer. He staggered forward a couple of steps, collapsed to his knees, then crumpled to his side on the hot sidewalk.

"Ehh . . . he's drunk," the tall man said with disgust. He hadn't noticed the way the driver's right arm dangled awkwardly, how his left hand clutched his sweat-stained shirt above his heart.

But *I* had.

"He's not drunk," I said. "He's having a heart attack!"

"Heart attack?" the tall man repeated.

By now a small crowd had gathered on the sidewalk.

"My God," exclaimed a woman in a yellow dress, pointing at the stricken man, "that's Harold Norquist!"

"Somebody do something!" a man with red hair shouted.

I was already on my knees beside the fallen man,

rolling him onto his back. I turned to the man in the straw hat. "Quick, go get a doctor," I yelled at him.

He just stood there, frozen.

"I'll go," Toni told me. She dashed back in the direction of the hospital.

I checked the man's pulse. There wasn't any. With alarm I noticed he was turning a horrible purplish white color.

"He's turning blue!" the woman in yellow screeched.

I checked his airway. The man had stopped breathing, too.

I knew what I had to do—having a dad who's also the chief of police has its benefits. Fortunately my CPR training was still current. Without a moment's hesitation I yanked the man's shirt open and began massaging his heart.

"What are you doing?" the red-haired man said. "Stop that—you'll kill him!"

Too late, I realized that it was decades before CPR had been invented—in 1972. No one had ever seen anyone do anything like this before. The skinny man tried to pull me off, but I shoved his hand away, hard. This man's life depended on my actions. "My father's a doctor," I lied. "I know what I'm doing!"

I raised the dying man's hands over his body, then brought them down again. Three quick breaths into the mouth. Then press three times. Then repeat.

"C'mon," I whispered, "breathe for me, buddy."

It wasn't looking good.

"You killed him," the red-haired man was saying. "You killed him!"

I ignored him, continuing with my first aid.

And then, like a miracle, the fat man coughed hard, twice, and began breathing. The color started to return to his face.

I sighed with relief.

By now Toni was approaching with Nurse Dreedle and an elderly physician. "What's that boy doing?" the doctor demanded. "Get him away from that man!"

As the doctor moved to take my place I was pushed to the outer edge of the crowd, where I was joined by Toni.

At the center of the group the fat man's eyes flickered open. "What happened?" he asked as the doctor pressed his stethoscope to his chest.

"You had a heart attack," the man in the straw hat explained.

"That strange boy saved your life," the woman in yellow added.

"Boy?" Mr. Norquist asked. "What boy? What are you talking about?"

"Why, the long-haired boy with the colored girl."

"*What* colored girl?" The man tried to sit up.

"Just you lie still now, Mayor Norquist," the

doctor said, pushing the big man back down on the pavement. "You're going to be fine."

Mayor Norquist?

Toni and I exchanged a worried glance.

"Uh-oh," she whimpered to me. "I think we might have just *unstepped* on a butterfly."

——— Chapter 7

Elena

The librarian came to our table, carrying three boxes full of tiny plastic canisters. "Here you are," she said, placing them down next to the microfilm viewer. She looked at Todd and me and smiled. "It's so nice to see children interested in learning, especially in the summertime."

As she walked away Todd let out a long, low groan. "Yeah, I'm interested in learning just how I got stuck in a library in July!" he complained.

"It's not so bad," I told him.

"Not so bad!" he exclaimed. Across the room the librarian shot us a dirty look.

Todd lowered his voice to a whisper. *"Not so bad?"* he repeated. The only other patrons were a gray-haired man slowly pecking at a laptop computer and a white-haired woman reading the latest large-type issue of *Reader's Digest.* "This is my idea of what hell looks like."

Ignoring him, I removed one of the plastic canisters from the box, examining its label.

METIER DAILY HERALD
JULY 1–15, 1945

65

"Look at it this way," I said, handing him the film. "The sooner we figure out what this Mason clue is, the sooner we get out of here."

"I suppose you're right," Todd said, flicking on the view screen. Uncapping the plastic case, he removed the spool of film, then threaded the film through the feeder. The screen was instantly filled with several columns of white-on-black text.

"We should check out the birth announcements first," I suggested. "See if there are any Masons born on July fifth."

Todd nodded, then pushed the button marked forward. With a hum the film began to advance. On-screen, the words became a rushing gray blur. After a couple of seconds Todd let go of the button, and the film stopped.

We had landed on an obituary page. There was a photo of a smiling, moon-faced man above the caption *Mayor Harold Norquist, Dead of Heart Attack at Age 57*.

I checked the date at the top of the screen. "'July sixth,'" I read. "You scrolled too far."

"Yeah, yeah, I can read," Todd said. He hit the button marked backward.

Nothing happened.

Todd hit the button a couple more times. Then he tried forward again.

No dice. The machine was stuck.

"Great!" Todd said in exasperation. "It's busted."

He pounded on the side of the monitor as if it were a TV with bad reception. "C'mon, you stupid piece of—" Whatever he was going to say, he never got it out.

"Todd?" I asked. "What's wrong?"

Todd was staring at the screen, his mouth hanging open.

I followed his gaze. It took me a moment to see what he was looking at. Then I gasped.

Harold Norquist's obituary was fading before our eyes! In a matter of seconds the words and photo had disappeared altogether, until there was nothing but a rectangular blank in the center of the screen.

Then, as the two of us watched in total shock, the rest of the articles on the page began rearranging themselves, rushing to fill in the gap where the death announcement had been.

Toni's mother's words came back to me: *Make a mistake in the past, and the universe tries to readjust itself to heal the damage you've caused.*

That's when I felt the first jolt. It seemed to come right through the floorboards under the table. "Did you feel that?" I asked Todd.

He nodded. "You don't think . . . ," he started.

Then the real rumbling began. *"Timequake!"* I screamed.

Todd grabbed my shoulder and we ducked under the desk. All around us shelves began to heave. Reference books and volumes of the encyclopedia came tumbling off the shelves. Plaster dust rained down from the old ceiling, joined by showers of glass as one by one the fluorescent lights exploded overhead. Was the whole building going to collapse?

Looking over, I could see the gray-haired man crouched under a nearby table, using his body to protect his laptop computer. The white-haired lady was lying facedown on the carpet, her *Reader's Digest* held over her head like a shield.

Then, just as suddenly as it started, the rumbling stopped. The last shards of glass tinkled to the floor. A final book fell to the carpet.

We weren't going to die after all.

"What the heck was that?" the old woman asked loudly, picking herself off the floor.

"It felt like an earthquake!" the gray-haired man responded, brushing some plaster dust off his computer.

"Earthquake?" the old lady screeched. "In the middle of *Wisconsin?*"

Just then the librarian reappeared. Her glasses dangled off one ear. "Would you all please keep your voices down?" she said disapprovingly. "Earthquake or not, this is *still* a library."

Chapter 8

Ashley

"Pay dirt!" Jack announced, holding the cordless phone over his head like a tomahawk.

"Give me a break," I muttered. This was the fourth time Jack had claimed to have hit "pay dirt." The first time had been a skateboarding company in New York City. The second time was a wrestling hot line in Butte, Montana. And the third number was, let's just say, not intended for anyone under twenty-one.

Now we were down to half a bag of potato chips, and we still had to try the number—JL5-1945—in twenty-six more area codes in the United States. Then it was time to start on the international calls.

"No, I mean it," he said, shoving the phone under my nose and hitting redial. "Check it out."

"Jack, I don't want to hear any more of your disgusting—wait a second!" I grew excited as I listened to the answering machine message. *"Hello,"* the man's voice said, *"you've reached Professor Mason Krieger in the science department of Madison University. I'm sorry I'm not here to take your call right now—"*

"This is the real thing!" I told Jack. "*Mason* Krieger. We've solved the puzzle!"

"Told ya," he said smugly.

Just then a live human voice picked up on the other end of the line. "Hello?" it said. "Hello?"

I covered the mouthpiece. "He's there!" I whispered.

"So?" Jack answered. "Why are you telling me? Talk to the guy!"

"What do I tell him?" I asked, panicking.

"How should I know?" Jack retorted. "Tell him you want to enroll in his classes. Tell him you're his long lost daughter. Tell him anything."

"Hello? Is anyone there?" came the voice through the phone.

I cleared my throat. "Excuse me, professor," I started, "I know this is going to sound a little strange, but, um, I have a problem I was hoping you might help me with." I was shooting for a dignified tone of voice, but I think I came out somewhere closer to desperate.

"Yes?" he replied. "What sort of problem?"

"Well," I stalled, "since you're a professor of, uh . . ."

"Genetics," he filled in.

"Genetics, right, well, the truth is, I have this sort of question about genetics—"

"Certainly. What's the question?"

I looked at Jack. He shrugged, which was not particularly helpful.

"Hello?" came the professor's voice again. "Are you still there?"

"Yes, I'm here," I said wearily. "You wouldn't happen to believe I'm your long lost daughter, would you?"

"Young lady, is this some kind of prank?"

"No! No. Honest. It's just . . ." Then I got an idea. "A friend and I are writing this paper on famous genetics professors in Wisconsin, and I was hoping that maybe we could interview you."

"Oh, my," he said. "I hate to disappoint you, young lady, but I'm afraid that not only am I incredibly *nonfamous*, but after tonight I'll no longer be in Wisconsin."

"What do you mean?" I asked.

"It's just that I'm leaving tonight for Washington, D.C.," he replied.

"Oh," I said, crestfallen. "When are you getting back?"

"That's just the thing," he replied. "I'm not coming back. I'm moving to our nation's capital to begin a new job. So, unless you want to conduct this interview over the phone—"

"He's leaving tonight!" I hissed to Jack with the mouthpiece covered. Then into the phone I continued, "No, no, we really want to do the interview in person so that we can, uh, take pictures. To be included in the report. In case it gets published."

There was a pause on the other end of the line.

"Pictures, huh? Well, if you'd like to come up to Madison, by all means, stop in and have a chat. I'll see if I can't find a comb. But I should warn you, my plane leaves at seven-thirty sharp."

Seven-thirty! That barely left us enough time to get to Madison, let alone figure out how to convince Dr. Mason Krieger to stop the Omegas from taking over the world. Still, it was the only shot we had.

"What about the others?" I asked Jack once I had hung up with the professor. "They're expecting to meet us back here tonight. When they don't find us, they're going to think something terrible has happened."

"Already taken care of," Jack replied. He showed me a piece of paper on which he'd written:

Mason is Dr. Krieger.
Gone to Madison U. Back soon.

"That's it?" I asked.

"If you want," he replied, "I could put it in a few other languages."

"Forget it," I said, taking the pen and paper from his hand. "Boys are impossible."

I wrote out a detailed explanation of what had happened and where we were heading, then placed it where our friends would be sure to find it. "There," I announced. "Done. Let's get going."

Jack grabbed the remaining snack food and we were off, running to catch the 2:14 bus to Madison . . . and save the universe.

_____ **Chapter 9**

Toni

"Where to now?" I asked Ethan as we hurried down Main Street, leaving the scene of Mayor Norquist's accident before we could inadvertently cause more damage. "Should we go check out another hospital?"

"No," he said glumly. "There's no point to it. Maybe our Mason will be born later tonight. Or maybe his parents didn't want to have him in a hospital—a lot of babies used to be born at home. We won't know until we check the birth records tomorrow."

"You know, Ethan," I said, "I've been thinking. Let's say we do find a baby named Mason who was born on the fifth of July. What are we supposed to do once we find him? Change his diaper?"

Ethan looked at me. "I never even thought of that."

"So maybe Mason _isn't_ someone's name after all."

"What else could it be?" he asked.

"Oh, I don't know. . . . The name of a diner, perhaps?" I pointed toward the end of the block.

There, on the corner, stood a diner. A neon sign

hung above the door, buzzing on and off, like a beacon:

MASON'S DINER

"You know, you just might have something there," Ethan told me, and grinned.

Ting-a-ling!
No sooner had the bell rung as we passed through Mason's front door than every head was turned our way.

Out on the street I'd almost been convinced that Ethan was right: People were just surprised by the way we looked. Ethan's long (for a boy) hair, his pump-action sneakers, both of our strange clothes.

But as we walked into the diner I noticed that people weren't really staring at Ethan, just at me. Oh, they would *glance* at Ethan. But the serious eyeball tango was reserved for the *Toni Douglas Show.*

Admittedly, back in Metier Junior High, no one *ever* looked at Ethan, whereas certain boys were known to run their bikes into trees trying to look at me. But there I could excuse their stares as simple appreciation for my dead-on fashion sense and perfect hair.

This was something else.

The diner was crowded. Luckily we spotted two empty seats near the center of the counter. Ethan sat on one. I was about to sit next to him when something at the far end of the restaurant caught my eye.

There, against the back wall, stood an old jukebox.

I suddenly had an idea. Call it a hunch.

"Do you have any change?" I asked Ethan excitedly. He looked confused until I nodded toward the jukebox and told him: "I want to play selection *J-L-5*."

He nodded and fished some coins out of his pocket. "Good thinking," he said, handing me an assortment of nickels, dimes, and quarters. "I'll save your seat."

Making my way to the back of the diner, I was certain that I had figured out the clue. I could just imagine that when I pushed the buttons J-L-5, some secret message would start to play—maybe Mr. Koto's voice telling us who our mysterious scientist was and where to find him!

I was so caught up in my daydream that I didn't see the leg shoot out from one of the booths as I passed. I tripped and fell to my knees. Coins scattered everywhere.

"Watch where you're goin'," a man's voice snickered.

I was about to apologize until I heard him mutter a word under his breath, followed by derisive laughter.

I froze, feeling a bitter chill run down my spine.

I glanced up at the man for the first time. He

75

looked like he was in his early twenties. Heavyset, with curly black hair and splotchy skin. His gray eyes were dull and cold and somehow reminded me of the eyes of a shark. There was another man in the booth with him. A skinny man with yellowish hair and equally unfriendly eyes.

From the way they both were looking at me, I knew I'd been tripped on purpose.

The blond man's eyes narrowed. "You lookin' at somethin', girlie?"

I felt the palms of my hands begin to tingle, an electric charge begin to build. . . .

But as much as I would have liked to teach the two of them a lesson—namely, don't mess with Toni Douglas—I knew it wasn't worth it. Besides, who could tell what unforeseen damage it might cause to the future?

Instead I took a deep breath, scooped up the rest of my change, and headed over to the jukebox.

Butterflies . . . butterflies, I repeated to myself along the way. *Don't step on the butterflies.*

The jukebox was a really old model, not at all like the modern CD-playing ones I was used to. This one had carved wooden panels, neon bubble lights, mother-of-pearl buttons, and a stained glass window in the front that revealed the record player inside. Seeberg Nickel Melodeon was painted in fancy gold letters on the front.

With a shiver of anticipation I dropped a nickel in the coin slot. Started pressing buttons.

J . . . L . . .

Before I could press 5, a meaty arm reached in front of me, blocking my way.

It was the shark-eyed man from the booth. "Sorry. This machine's broke," he said. Behind him, his skinny blond friend snickered.

I held my ground. "It looks okay to me," I said, reaching around his arm and quickly pressing the 5 button.

Through the jukebox window I watched as the mechanical arm selected a disk, dropping it onto the turntable. It started spinning. The needle was lowered, music started to play—

And then the machine went dark.

Then I saw why: The blond man had pulled the plug.

"Nope," the shark-eyed man repeated. "It's definitely broke. Now why don't you leave."

They called me a name again.

And suddenly I didn't care so much about protecting the future.

It's time for Toni Douglas to step on some butterflies.

I smiled my sweetest smile. "But I don't want to leave," I said, placing one hand on the jukebox. "And I still think you're mistaken about this machine."

I concentrated, focusing all my energy through my palm, willing life into the jukebox. There was a humming sound, and the box suddenly lit up again—ten times brighter. The record started spinning, and a young girl's shrill voice sang out at an earache-causing pitch:

"On the goo-oo-ood ship Lol-lee Pop! It's a swee-ee-eet trip to the can-dee shop!"

Well, I guess J-L-5 wasn't Mr. Koto after all. But it sure had the right effect.

The skinny blond guy stared at the pulled plug in his hand, then at the phantom jukebox, which was crackling with pink electricity. "What the—how is that—what are you—?" he stammered.

"Where bonbons plaaaaay on the sunny shore of Peppermint Baaaaay!"

His shark-eyed friend was having an equal reaction. "It's—it's possessed!" he squealed. "Let's get out of here!"

And before you could say, "Bye-bye, bigots"—

Ting-a-ling! Ting-a-ling!

—the two of them had disappeared out the diner's front door.

Once those two jerks had been frightened off, I was finally able to join Ethan for a meal of huge cheeseburgers and fries. The waitress looked at me funny when I ordered a diet Coke, but she had no problem once I changed my order to a chocolate malted. I figured I deserved it—it's not every day that I defeat a couple of racist pigs. Besides, my little exercise in audio electronics had left me with a major appetite.

Of course, I was bummed that my hunch about the jukebox had been wrong and that selection JL5 hadn't been anything more than that dumb Shirley Temple song.

"We don't know that for sure," Ethan said, sucking down the last of his root beer float. "I mean, maybe this Mason person works in a candy shop and plays with bonbons."

I laughed. "Or lives on the sunny shore of Peppermint Bay?"

Our waitress came over. "Would you like anything else?" she asked.

We shook our heads no. "Just the check, please," I said.

She scribbled on her pad, then tore off the top sheet. "That comes to ninety-five cents," she said, placing the bill down on the counter.

Ninety-five cents?

Once she was far enough away, Ethan and I broke out into shocked laughter.

"That's *it?*" I said. "You mean all that food cost less than a dollar?"

"Wow," Ethan said, counting out a dollar's worth of change. "Maybe when this is all over, we should come and live here for good." He plunked down a couple of quarters more for the tip.

"No, thank you," I replied. After all the trouble I'd attracted today, I wanted to be as far away from here as possible. Those two racist jerks.

Practically made me homesick for the giant rats.

We were almost out the door when our waitress screamed, "Stop!"

We spun around. "What's the matter?" Ethan said. "Didn't we leave enough tip?"

"Sure—if I could pay my rent in play money. Just what kind of coins *are* these?" she said. She held them out to one of the diners, a strong-looking guy in overalls. "Look at the dates on these coins, Vince—1981 . . . 1979 . . . 1997! Why, they're all fakes! And these dimes—who is this man supposed to be?"

"It looks like President Roosevelt!" said the man in overalls.

That's because it is Franklin Roosevelt, I thought with a sick twisting in my gut. *Only he won't appear on a dime until 1946 . . . a whole year away.*

"Counterfeiters!" the waitress yelled, scooping up the phone and starting to dial. "Lock the door, Vince, and don't let them leave. I'm calling the police!"

Chapter 10

Jack

"Do you think Dr. Krieger's going to be mad?" I asked Ashley as we walked across the giant lawn that spread between the brick buildings of Madison University.

"You mean will he be *angry* at us?"

"No," I clarified. "I mean will he be bonkers."

Ashley shot me an annoyed look. "What are you talking about, Jack?"

"Well, he's a genetics scientist. That's like Dr. Frankenstein, right?" I could picture him now: bug eyes, white hair like a mop head, cackling maniacally as he sloshed bubbling green liquid from one test tube to another.

"He sounded normal enough on the phone," Ashley replied.

"Aw, come on, Ash," I teased. "Admit it. I bet Krieger's lying to us about the Washington job. He's *really* leaving town to escape the angry villagers with torches who are going to burn his lab to the ground."

Ashley rolled her eyes. "Whatever you say, Jack."

81

We had reached the far end of the square, where a group of pretty college girls were standing around a tall ladder. They were hanging a huge paper banner between two trees. "Excuse me," I asked one of them, a perky-looking blond. "Do you know where we can find Professor Krieger?"

"Do you know what department he's in?" she asked.

"Science," Ashley answered.

"Hmmm." The blond thought a second, then turned to another girl in the group. "Kelly—you're a bio major. Do you know a Professor Krieger?"

"Krieger?" replied a redhead in glasses. She shook her head. "Sorry. Never heard of him. But that's the science building over there," she told us, nodding toward one of the ivy-covered structures.

"You must be the students doing the report," said a friendly voice as soon as we passed through the huge brass doors of the science building. "I'm Dr. Krieger," he said, extending his hand.

To my great disappointment, Dr. Krieger turned out to be a perfectly normal-looking guy of about forty. His light brown hair was thinning, and he wore horn-rimmed glasses. He didn't even have the decency to wear a lab coat. Instead he was dressed in a light blue polo shirt and khaki pants. If he *was* mad, he was certainly doing a good job of keeping it to himself.

He shook our hands. "Come," he said, smiling, "let me take you to my office."

We followed Dr. Krieger down a carpeted hallway, past college kids in T-shirts and sandals who shuttled back and forth between work cubicles. He led us down a flight of stairs, through another hallway, down a *second* flight of stairs, and finally into his basement-level office.

No wonder that girl Kelly hadn't known him, I thought. Dr. Krieger's office was so hidden away, you practically needed a compass to find it. "Where are all the test tubes and body parts and the thing that makes sparks?" I demanded once we'd entered the dimly lit room.

"Never mind Jack," Ashley said. "He hasn't taken his medication today."

"No, no," the professor said, "he's just showing a healthy curiosity. Well, Jack, I'm afraid I do most of my work on computers, not dead bodies. As for my equipment—it's all packed up, ready to come with me to Washington."

We were surrounded by packing cartons of every shape and size, from big ones that looked like they held half a library to smaller ones marked Fragile and Treat Like Glass.

"Are you going there to teach at another university?" Ashley asked.

"No," he replied. "I'm going to work for the government. They've offered to fund my research in an exciting new area, called IGF—interspecies genetic fusion. Combining the genes of different animals to create new organisms."

Ashley and I exchanged a knowing glance. "That's very . . . interesting," I said.

"Oh, it's much more than interesting," he replied. "It's like a dream come true. I can finally do the experiments I've been waiting to perform all my life."

"Why do you suppose the government is interested in genetics?" Ashley asked.

"They didn't tell me," he said with a smile, "and I didn't ask. You know, 'Don't look a gift horse in the mouth' and all that."

"But what if the government had something . . . *sinister* in mind for your research?" I asked.

The professor blinked a couple of times. "I'm not sure I know what you mean."

"Jack," Ashley whispered, "go *slow*. We're trying to convince the professor, not scare him."

"Convince me?" Dr. Krieger said. "Convince me of what, exactly?"

I turned back to the balding man. "Professor Krieger, let's say, theoretically, that you were visited by someone from the distant future."

The professor's eyebrows raised, then he chuckled. "Okay . . . ," he said.

Ashley was watching me closely. I smiled back at her, as if to say, *See, I can handle this.*

"And let's say," I continued, "that this person told you that in the future, the human race had been totally wiped out in a devastating struggle against genetically engineered monsters that the government had developed using your technique, except for a few people, who were forced to live underground, battling giant rats. What would you tell them?"

Ashley groaned. The professor just stared at me. "Is this part of the interview?" he asked.

Ashley clamped her hand over my mouth. "Professor Krieger, this is going to strike you as very hard to believe, but we know how your work is going to turn out. We've seen the future. And even though you may not think your work can be used for evil, we're here to tell you that it will be."

"Oh, but you're wrong," he protested. "My research is harmless."

"It is right now," Ashley told him. "But in a few years the government is going to realize that your research has military applications. They'll use it to create genetically enhanced soldiers. Horrible killing machines who will destroy the earth as we know it."

"If you go to Washington tonight," I concluded, "you'll be signing a death warrant on humankind."

Professor Krieger looked back and forth from Ashley to me, as if he were trying to tell if we were pulling his leg. "Let me get this straight. You're asking me to abandon my life's work . . . because you have a scary story about the future?" He laughed. "That's the most ridiculous thing I've ever heard in my life."

I'd had a feeling he was going to react this way. That's why I'd come prepared. "Ridiculous, huh?" I asked, removing a safety pin from my pocket. "And how ridiculous is *this?*"

I jabbed the point into the tip of my index finger.

"What are you *doing?*" the professor shouted. But then he fell silent.

A drop of my blood was beginning to form where I'd pricked the tip of my index finger.

It was silver.

It hung there, like a perfect globule of mercury. I could see the professor's face reflected in it as his jaw dropped to the floor. "Who—what—who *are* you?" he stammered.

"We're the results of your experiment, Professor," I replied. "And the future of the world depends on your assistance. Are you with us or against us?"

He stared at us for what seemed like hours.

"With you," he replied.

Chapter 11

Ethan

When the two police officers arrived at Mason's Diner, they wasted no time in confiscating our "counterfeit" money, cuffing us, and leading us out to their waiting patrol cars.

Outside, the diner was bathed in a flashing red glow from the patrol car's "cherry," the revolving red light on the car's roof. Apparently in 1945 they hadn't yet thought of adding blue and white lights, like my dad had on his car. "Watch your head," the patrolman said as he ushered Toni into the back of the police cruiser. She shot him a sassy look, then bumped her forehead on the door frame.

In the minutes before the cops showed up, Toni and I discussed the possibilities of escape. Apparently her little jukebox show had drained her too much. Even after eating, she still didn't feel like she had enough juice to time-jump both of us away. I suppose I could have started fighting and maybe even have gotten away, but that wouldn't have helped Toni, who was the real ticket out of here.

Now Toni thunked down next to me, looking

like she wished there was someone *she* could punch out. "I can't believe this," she growled. "What else can go wrong?"

"Well, look at it this way," I told her. "We needed a place to stay until you could recharge, and now we have one. Besides, what do they even have on us? Some fake-looking dimes and nickels. They probably won't even stick us in jail. They'll probably just fingerprint us, take our pictures, and let us go."

"I hope you're right," she said. "I do *not* want to spend the night in jail."

In fact, I was a lot less certain than I sounded. Counterfeiting was a major crime. I wasn't sure about the laws in the 1940s, but in the 1990s the FBI got involved in counterfeiting cases. In a small town like Metier, this was going to get some serious attention. Not what we needed.

As we drove off, I watched Mason's Diner disappear in the rear window. We rounded the corner onto Fillmore, and I noticed a second patrol car screech to a stop outside the restaurant.

I had no idea what we'd say once we reached the station. There were all kinds of questions that we couldn't answer. How could we possibly explain where we'd gotten the money? To make matters worse, we were minors—where were our parents?

"This is kind of interesting," Toni said. She was holding her cuffed wrist up to the light.

"What's that?" I asked.

"Look at these weird handcuffs. They aren't chrome, like the ones we have in the nineties. They're a lot bigger. And the chain connecting them is much heavier. It's iron or something."

"I guess that's how they made them in 1945," I replied.

I noticed Toni's lip was quivering. "Toni," I asked, concerned, "are you okay?"

"What's wrong with my life?" she wailed. "I'm only thirteen, and this is my second time in the back of a police car!" She wiped her nose against her shirtsleeve. "I'm, like, the world's only eighth grader who's an authority on handcuffs!"

"Toni," I whispered, "come on. Pull it together. They're going to hear you."

As if on cue, the policeman behind the wheel turned around. He peered at us through the metal grid that separated the front seat from the back. "So, what are you two dressed up for—a circus?" he asked.

His partner in the passenger seat laughed as if he'd just heard the best joke in human history.

"If we are," Toni muttered under her breath, "I certainly know where we can find the clowns."

I chuckled silently. Then the laughter caught in my throat.

A lot had changed in Metier since 1945, but the police station hadn't. I remembered my dad showing me a plaque on the wall that commemorated the station's founding, back in 1910. They just had two police officers back then—a sheriff and a deputy—and instead of a cruiser they used a horse-drawn carriage. But since the day it was founded, seventy-five years before my birth, the police station had always been in the same two-story brick building on Main Street.

So why were they taking us out toward the reservoir?

It couldn't be. They *couldn't* be Omegas. It was 1945! How would they even know to look for us here?

That patrol car I saw squeal up to the diner—I suddenly realized they weren't backup after all. They were the *real* police officers arriving at the scene. That meant the officers driving this car were . . . something else.

I get sick to my stomach when I'm watching a horror movie and the hero is about to go into the house where the killer is waiting. I was getting that same feeling now. I peered into the rearview mirror, trying to get a glimpse of the officers' faces. Maybe I'd be wrong.

I leaned forward, looking at the necks of the two men in the front seat in their stiff, blue 1945 patrolman uniforms. They sure didn't look like Omegas. Maybe this was all in my imagination. But I had to be sure.

I leaned back nonchalantly and turned to Toni. "Actually," I informed her, "I think I know why they decided to replace the old iron handcuffs with chrome ones. My dad told me once. The old handcuffs were too easy to break if they'd been *heated up.*"

She looked at my expression and caught my emphasis on the words *heated up.* "Are we in some kind of danger?" she whispered. Then I think she made the same calculations I just had. "Are they—?" she asked.

I nodded silently.

"What are you kids talking about back there?" the policeman in the passenger seat asked. He chuckled. "You aren't planning on trying to make a break for it, are you?"

"I was just noticing that if you're trying to get to the police station, you've got an awfully roundabout way of doing it," I told him.

"How do you mean?" he asked.

"I mean that the police station isn't in this direction," I replied, "not even in 1945."

"You're smart," his partner said. "Maybe a little too smart."

With a violent tug on the wheel the driver swung the car into a side street that ended in an alleyway. He parked the car and jumped out. Then he came around back and opened the door.

The charade was over. As we watched, his features started to morph. The bones of his face began to rearrange themselves. His skin stretched and turned silvery. He grew taller, thinner, until his features had gelled into the form of an Omega assassin.

"Get out of the car," the creature ordered, its obsidian eyes radiating with barely contained rage. "Now." It had a nightstick in one hand and the hilt of a service revolver in the other.

"Make me," said Toni, holding out her handcuffed wrists.

The creature snarled with what might have been a laugh. "My pleasure."

He grabbed the handcuffs by the chain, intending to yank Toni headfirst out of the car. I guess he hadn't seen the tiny sparks arcing around the surface of the handcuffs like hundreds of small pink fireflies.

"*Aaaaaugh!*" the Omega screamed as seventy thousand volts of pure energy shot up his arms. He fell to the ground, spasming with the force of the blow. His hand had burned through the chain link on Toni's handcuffs.

"Run, Toni!" I shouted as she leaped from the car. "Go! Go!"

"We'll see how far she gets," the other Omega snarled, sliding into the driver's seat. With a vicious twist of his wrist he turned over the ignition and slammed the car into gear. The patrol car's wheels squealed as he burned rubber down the alleyway.

Toni looked back over her shoulder, squinting into the oncoming headlights. She had only a moment to think. There was nowhere to run—and the car was moving like a black-and-white blur.

"You can't kill her!" I shouted. "You need her—you need us alive!"

"Be quiet, Alpha scum," the Omega hissed. "Alive or dead, it's all the same now."

We were headed straight at a brick wall. Toni was trapped against it. There were only seconds until impact. Even if I could have grabbed the wheel, it would accomplish nothing—she would still die.

But as it turned out, I didn't have to help her. Suddenly there was a brilliant flash, and Toni was gone.

As the brick wall came at us at seventy miles an hour, I wished that I knew the same trick. I clutched the seat in front of me, bracing myself for impact. But I knew it was over. There was no way I could live through the crash.

————— Chapter 12

Ashley

The professor had his head between his hands, looking at us in shock. We had just told him the entire story of the Omega project. How his research had been corrupted for military purposes. How the Alphas, genetically engineered to be the perfect fighting machines, had developed consciences and broken free of the government enclosure. How the Omegas, built to correct the "flaws" in the Alpha project, had turned against the very people who made them. And how our parents, survivors of the Alpha project, had been betrayed by one of their own, forced to fight the Omegas through us, their children.

"So if I had left for Washington tonight," he said finally, "that would have been the end of it." He sighed heavily. "The end of mankind."

"Yes," I replied. "But look at the bright side. We found you in time."

"I hope you're right." The professor seemed lost in thought for a second. Then he studied us carefully. "But let's be careful about this. We can't have any loose ends."

"What kind of loose ends?" I asked.

"Well, I suppose I can destroy all my notes and research, but I can't erase my memory. Someone still might come for me and force me to repeat my studies. That's why I'll have to hide out for a while. Maybe a long time. If there's any way I can be found, the planet could still be in danger." His eyes flashed with concern. "Who knows that you've come here to warn me?"

"No one," Jack said. "We had to come in such a hurry, all we could do was leave a note for our friends."

"That's good," the professor replied. "The less outside involvement, the better. Aside from the note, did you write my name down anywhere, in a diary or a letter to a friend, perhaps?"

"No," I told him. "We've been too busy to do anything but try to figure out our next move."

"Yes," he said sympathetically. "You do look exhausted. Finally, what about the other Alpha children? As long as they're still out there, they could reveal my name or be in danger themselves. Do you know where they are now?"

"Well, two of them are at the public library in Metier," I replied. "The other two are looking for you back in July 1945. But they'll probably come here once they find our note in the tree house."

"I see," Professor Krieger said. He took off his horn-rimmed glasses, put them into his pocket, and stood up. "Let me tell you what we're going to do. I have some friends who live out of town. We'll stay at their place for a few days. I'm going to call the people in Washington and tell them that I've been delayed. That'll buy us some time without arousing their suspicions."

The professor walked over to the door, then stopped and looked back at us. "In the meantime, try to think if there's anything you've forgotten. Anymore loose ends that could lead our enemies here."

He shut the door behind him quietly, leaving Jack and me alone in the empty office. "Gee," Jack said, "do you think I should have told him about the bread crumbs?"

"What bread crumbs?" I asked.

"The ones I've been dropping since we left the gingerbread house," he answered.

"Jack, for once in your life, try to be serious."

"Okay, I'll be serious. There's something wrong with that guy. I don't like him."

The truth was, I was thinking the same thing. In the movies, whenever someone starts asking you about "loose ends"—like whether you've told anyone else where a treasure is hidden, for instance—it's usually because they're about to kill you and take the treasure for themselves. But that was just in the movies. We had every reason to trust Professor Krieger. Everything he said and did made sense. And in any case, there was no way I was going to give Jack the satisfaction of knowing that I secretly thought he was right. "Well, I'm sure he's not too crazy about you, either," I shot back.

"I'm serious, Ash. Doesn't he seem a little strange?"

"You should know, Jack. You're the resident expert on strange."

"Why was he asking us all those questions?"

"Weren't you paying attention? He was trying to figure out if anyone could trace us here. Anyone who'd want to hurt us."

"Or help us," he added.

"Oh, come on!" I protested. "Krieger's on our side! And we need him, Jack. We need him to defeat the Omegas." I crossed my arms and sat down heavily on one of the cardboard boxes. To my total humiliation, it crumpled under my weight.

Jack snickered. "Let's hope its contents weren't breakable," he said. "Or radioactive."

"This isn't funny," I told him, opening the box carefully. "I hope he doesn't come in and see us like this." I lifted the cardboard flaps gingerly. What I saw inside took my breath away.

It was empty.

"Jack," I said, a tingling feeling of cold dread creeping over my body, "look at this."

Jack peered into the box. "Wow," he said, "he really packs light."

I lifted the box closest to me. I could immediately tell by the weight that there was nothing inside it, either. "This one's empty, too," Jack announced, holding a third box over his head.

"They're *all* empty," I realized in horror. "Jack, what does this mean?"

"One of two things," Jack replied. "Either he studies gases and this is his oxygen collection, or—"

"Or?" I prompted.

"Or we're going to have to figure out a way to get out that window," he replied. "Because he's right outside in the hall, and by now I'm sure he's not alone."

I looked at the window in question, a pane of clouded glass maybe two feet long and ten inches high. It looked more like a mail slot than a window. Plus it was a good eight feet off the ground. How were we ever going to fit through *that?*

Professor Krieger returned to the room a few instants later. For a moment, I thought we'd made a terrible mistake and this mild-mannered scientist was going to be convinced once and for all that we were totally crazy.

When he didn't see us, he froze in his tracks. "Children?" he called out, frowning.

Then he noticed the boxes we'd stacked up to reach the window, which was now standing wide open. In two swift strides he had crossed to the makeshift stairs. His face contorted in rage. With a ferocious growl the professor lashed out, sending the boxes flying. He raised his fist and spoke into his wristwatch.

"They've escaped!" he snarled, dropping his disguise. In an instant his eyes grew wider, darker, morphing into the horrible black orbs of an Omega. "Search the grounds! They couldn't have gotten far." He turned and ran out into the hallway.

The minute the coast was clear, Jack and I emerged from our hiding place inside one of the huge packing crates. "It's a good thing he fell for that," Jack commented. "I hear the backs of those UPS vans are very uncomfortable."

"Come on!" I whispered. "Let's get out of here!"

Moments later we were retracing our path away from the fake professor's office.

We exited the stairwell onto the main floor of the science building. It was empty now; the students were gone. We crept quickly along the carpeted hallway, past the cubicles with their dark computer screens, finally arriving at the large brass doors. Hopefully our trick had worked. If the Omegas believed we'd already escaped through the back window, they wouldn't be watching the front entrance. Holding our breath, we pushed open the huge doors.

Outside, the campus square looked empty.

We ran out into the warm night air and were about to bolt across the wide lawn when I realized that something was very, very wrong.

I looked up—and screamed in terror.

There in the night sky was the Omegas' time machine, a huge metallic sphere that hung in the darkness like a deadly silver moon. A ring of blue lights pulsed on its underside like an alien heartbeat. The humming of its main drive drowned out all other sound.

For a terrible second I was paralyzed, unable to move or even breathe.

Then all at once the spell was broken. I realized the full horror of our situation. We couldn't be taken prisoner, not again. But running across the open field would be useless. We'd be sitting ducks.

Instead we turned back toward the science building.

As we dashed toward the entrance a funny sensation came over me. All at once the air around me felt funny. Thicker and . . . *staticky*. It felt as if I was trying to run through a swimming pool—a pool filled with honey. What was happening?

Then I looked down at my feet, and my heart almost stopped dead in my chest: I was hanging six inches off the ground.

The Omega craft had caught me in a tractor beam!

I started rising, feetfirst, into the air.

"Jack!" I screamed.

He spun to look back at me. His eyes grew wide in astonishment and fear. Too late, he held out his hand. I made a desperate lunge for his arm, but my fingertips merely grazed his.

Then, as I watched in horror, Jack began rising, too.

We rose right past the banner that the college girls had been hanging earlier. *Pledge Delta Delta Mu! The Deltas Want You!* it read in large red letters. As we floated past, Jack grabbed hold of the flimsy paper sign. I managed to grab onto his ankle.

For a moment we were suspended there like some crazy, upside-down mobile. Jack strained against the force of the tractor beam, even though we both knew it was a losing battle.

I glanced up at the hovering ship and shuddered at the thought of what was waiting for us inside. We had fought so hard to get this far—and now it was all for nothing.

With a horrible ripping noise the banner was torn loose, and Jack and I were sailing through the open air.

The Deltas might want us, I thought miserably.

But the Omegas have *us*.

———— Chapter 13

Elena

"Fifteen minutes to closing, children," said the librarian. She no longer looked glad to see young minds engaged in the pursuit of knowledge. Now she just looked like she wanted us to leave.

"Have you found any leads?" I asked Todd, who was tapping keys at one of the library's computers, surrounded by thick reference books. It was funny. After he got past his initial grumbling, Todd seemed to like this kind of detective work. It looked like he was pretty good at it, too. "Anything to go on?"

Todd stopped typing. "I've cross-indexed the town historical archives with phone books, school records, anything that might give us information," he said dejectedly.

"No Masons?" I asked.

"The opposite," he replied. "*Thousands* of them. Towns. Cities. Factories. Businesses. Home owners. Little kids. Senior citizens. All named Mason."

"I guess it's a popular name," I offered lamely.

Todd groaned. "We've been here all day, and we've got nothing to show for it." He threw down his pencil in disgust. "I don't understand it!"

Something was bothering me, too. I couldn't shake the feeling that the answer was right here, somewhere in this very building, hidden among the stacks of old books. It was staring us in the face, I was sure of it. And as I knew from past experience, my hunches had the habit of coming true.

"We can come back in the morning," I reminded him.

"I guess," he replied sourly. "If the Omegas haven't captured us by then."

Just as he finished saying the words, we heard the sound of the front door to the library being flung open. Someone was coming to the library at this late hour? From the next room we heard the librarian warn someone, "We're closing in fifteen minutes." But who was she saying it to?

Todd and I looked at each other with the same thought on our minds: an Omega assassin? The reference room had no windows and no fire doors. We were trapped. "Get ready to make a break for it," he said.

When the late night visitor appeared around the corner, I could have laughed with relief.

"Toni! What are you doing here?" I asked her as she collapsed into the chair next to Todd. Something was obviously wrong. She was breathing heavily and looked like she was about to cry. "What's the matter?"

"They got him," she stammered. "They got Ethan."

"What do you mean?" Todd asked. "Who's got Ethan?"

"The Omegas," she replied. "They were there waiting for us. I got away. Ethan didn't."

"Is he . . . dead?" I asked.

"I don't know," she replied. "They were trying to run me down. They had Ethan in the car. I was cornered in an alley with a brick wall behind me, and the car was doing, like, a hundred miles an hour. Just before it hit me, I managed to jump out of there." She paused, her lip quivering. "If anything happened to him, I don't know what I'll do."

"Wait a second," Todd cut in. "You guys were in *1945!* How did the Omegas even know you two were there?"

"That's just what we thought!" Toni said. "I'm like, 'It makes no sense. They shouldn't be here.' But you can't argue with a seven-foot black-eyed freak."

"In police work," Todd commented, "when an undercover operation goes bad or when the criminals are always one step ahead of you, it usually means one of two things. One, that there's a traitor in your midst."

"I think we can rule that one out," I said. "What's option two?"

"That we've been bugged," Todd replied.

"Bugged?" Toni repeated. "But how? When? Where?"

A sickening thought entered my mind. "Oh my God," I said, turning to Todd. "You and me . . . we were asleep in the Omegas' tanks for months. Who *knows* what they might have done to us." I put a hand on my stomach, suddenly feeling ill. "Maybe they placed a bug . . . *inside us.*"

"Maybe . . . but I don't think so," Todd said. "If the bug were on you or me, why would we both still be here? The Omegas would've gotten us by now, right?" He frowned, rubbing his chin. "No, my guess is that they tapped our families' phone lines, thinking we might try to call our parents once we came back."

"But we *haven't* called them!" Toni pointed out. "Ethan told us not to."

"You're right," Todd agreed. "We haven't called them. But Jack and Ashley have been using his parents' phone all day long—"

"—and the Omegas were probably listening in the whole time!" I slammed the table in frustration. "How could we have been so stupid?"

"We have to warn them!" Toni said, her eyes wide.

"It might be too late for that," Todd added ominously.

Toni was already digging in her shorts for a quarter. "There's a pay phone outside. Do either of you know Jack's number?"

"Don't bother," I told her. "I have a faster way than phoning."

I closed my eyes and concentrated. It had been a while since I'd tried doing this, and for a second I was afraid I wouldn't remember how. But I suppose astral projection is a lot like seeing Jack Raynes perform his tribute to the Spice Girls in the seventh-grade talent show: something I could never forget. Even if I wanted to.

Using my mind, I pushed down and *up* . . . and suddenly I was floating above the library table, looking down at Todd and Toni and my own, physical body, which I'd left below. I watched as it slumped to one side, seemingly asleep.

The scene below disappeared as my spirit passed right through the ceiling of the reference room. For a brief moment I was inside the library's dark, cobwebby attic, then I emerged through the shingled roof and into the open, starry sky.

Above me, the full moon cast a silver glow on the trees and rooftops. For a second I was taken by how beautiful my little town looked.

Then like a streak of light, I raced toward Jack's tree house.

Five minutes later I was back.

"Well?" Todd asked. "Were they there?"

I shook my head, still a little woozy from my recent flight. "No—but Ashley left a note. They went to see a professor named Mason Krieger at Madison University," I informed them. "He was leaving tonight, so they had to hurry up there without consulting us."

"He just happened to be moving to another city *tonight?*" Todd wondered. "That sounds suspicious to me."

"Me too," Toni added. "Let's go call his office. If they arrived safely, great. If not . . ."

She didn't have to finish her thought. Digging in our pockets, we rounded up a stack of change—Madison is a long-distance call—then hurried toward the exit.

Suddenly the ground lurched, the room started spinning, and I went careening into one of the bookshelves. At first I thought we were in the midst of another timequake, until I noticed that no one but me was affected. I was having one of my dizzy spells—the kind that accompanied a psychic premonition—like when I saw the rats.

What were my powers trying to warn me of this time? Were the Omegas coming?

My vision had grown blurry. I grabbed onto the shelf to steady myself, bracing for the flash of the future, my mystical glimpse into the soon-to-be-now.

But it never came.

Instead my vision simply cleared, and I was staring at a neat row of library books. Or, more specifically, at their spines. Or, even *more* specifically—*at the answer to our clue.*

I whirled around to face Todd and Toni, who were already halfway out the door. "Guys, wait!" I called after them. "It's a call number!"

"What?" Todd said, coming back into the library. "*What's* a call number?"

"JL5.1945. It's a call number for a book. Just follow the Dewey decimal system!"

There was no time to spare. Toni went on ahead to the pay phone while Todd and I stayed behind, frantically scanning the library shelves for the JL section. It turned out to be the genetics and genetic-engineering section. It seemed like it was a popular subject—there were dozens of books to go through. We'd have to get lucky. There was no way that we could look through all of them before—

"The library is closed," said a voice so close behind us that I jumped. It was the librarian, looking like she wasn't going to take "no"—or even "maybe"—for an answer. She buttoned a pink shawl around her neck as if to say, *Let's go.* "Why don't you come back tomorrow during our normal hours?"

"We just need a few more moments," I pleaded. "It's very important."

"I'm sorry," the librarian said. "But if I made an exception for you and let you stay late, I'd have to let everybody stay late."

I looked around. As far as I could tell, we were the only ones crazy enough to want to stay this long. But I knew that argument wasn't going to sway the woman standing in front of me.

"I've got it! Positive ID!" Todd yelled suddenly. He was holding up a book called *Advances in Recombinant Genetics*, by Alice Mason, Ph.D.

Moments later we were standing at the checkout desk as the librarian reluctantly punched our card. "I hope this is what you were looking for," she said, handing us the book. "Have a good night."

You didn't have to be psychic to hear the words she wanted to add: *and don't ever come back.*

As we walked to the convenience store to pick up Toni, I read through the information on the back jacket. "If this isn't another trap, it's got to be what Mr. Koto wanted us to find," I told Todd.

"There's nothing that says it can't be both," Todd pointed out. "Maybe the aliens have figured out what Mr. Koto had in mind and they've sent assassins to cover all the bases."

"That's a chance we have to take," I replied. "We're out of choices. Listen to this." I read from the jacket cover. "'Dr. Alice Mason received her doctorate degree in genetics from the University of Kent in England. She lives and carries out her research in Metier, Wisconsin.'"

"I don't know," Todd said. "It still sounds too perfect. We have to have a backup plan in case it's a trap."

When we reached the convenience store, Toni was standing in front, pacing nervously. "What's the matter?" I asked, although I knew what she was going to say.

"I tried the number, but it was disconnected. So then I called the university information desk," she told us. "They've got no listing for a Professor Mason Krieger. As far as they know, he doesn't exist." She looked worried. "Guys, this could be *seriously* bad."

"Wherever Ashley and Jack are," I said, "we can be sure of one thing. They're not in Wisconsin anymore."

_____Chapter 14

Ethan

Being held captive in an Omega ship is frustrating enough. My friends and I were suspended in thick plastic tubes filled with yellow fluid like specimens on display in a tent of circus oddities. Without help, I knew, there was no way out. None of my super-powers would help me here.

But what was really frustrating was that I had to listen to my Omega captors make plans, plans that spelled my friends' doom, and I was utterly power-less to do anything about it.

The ironic thing was, I had gotten lucky. There was every chance that I would have been killed in the car crash. When Toni jumped, the police cruiser had no time to stop. We would have smashed into the brick wall, doing more than seventy miles an hour.

But thanks to the Omega's sophisticated technol-ogy, the entire police car was sucked up into the night sky by their time ship's tractor beam.

I was fine. Fine, of course, except for being the captive of a group of creatures that wanted to de-stroy me and my entire race.

Which is what they were planning to do right now, just outside my plastic prison.

The Omegas' leader—identified by his silver uniform—was addressing an Omega spy on one of the many view screens that lined the walls.

"We have deciphered Alpha-Eight's clue," the spy reported. "If the remaining Alpha offspring have figured it out as well, then we shall be there, waiting for them."

"Good," the leader said. "Remember: You must be careful. Everything rests on your success. Everything."

If that was true, then everything depended on my warning my friends. Somehow I had to get free. But how?

_____ Chapter 15

Todd

We decided not to waste any time before finding Dr. Mason. After all, her address was right here in town. Yes, it was late. But I figured that once we explained to her that the fate of humanity was at stake, she'd understand.

We arrived at the tiny row house on the outskirts of town just after ten o'clock. According to the book jacket, this was where Dr. Mason did all her research. To our surprise, the lights were still on inside.

"I guess Dr. Mason's a night owl," I speculated.

"That or she forgot to turn out the lights," Toni replied.

As we walked closer to the lab I noticed something. "She forgot something else," I added. "She forgot to close the door." I pointed to the yellow light, spilling from the open door into the inky night.

"I don't like the looks of this," Toni whispered as we walked up the short landing to the front door.

"Me either," Elena said. "Do you think someone got here ahead of us?"

Slowly we eased open the door.

"Well," I said, "either that, or Dr. Mason is an even worse slob than Jack."

The place was a total wreck. Broken test tubes littered the floor. Metal struts, petri dishes, and battered scientific equipment were strewn everywhere. In one corner a smashed-up computer shot out sparks like a bug zapper.

This wasn't random vandalism. The damage was deliberate. Someone *purposely* wrecked this lab. But why?

"Whoever you are, you're too late," a voice said sadly.

We whirled around to see a woman in her midthirties standing stock-still to one side of the room. She was wearing a white lab coat, her ash blond hair pulled back in a loose ponytail.

The first thing I noticed was that Dr. Alice Mason was much prettier in person than in the photo on her book jacket.

The second thing I noticed about her was that she was holding a strange rock in her hands.

"What happened here?" Elena asked.

"Maybe I'll explain. But first let's step inside my apartment and close the shades."

Dr. Mason's apartment was right next door to her lab—a nice arrangement, I supposed, if your life is your work and vice versa. She seated us around her kitchen table, putting a pot of water on the stove for tea.

By the time the teakettle whistled, we'd filled her in on as much as we knew. She listened silently to our fantastic story of Alphas, superpowers, and future apocalypses. By the time we finished, she sat there wide-eyed, looking a bit skeptical.

There seemed to be a communication problem, and I knew just how to solve it.

"Dr. Mason, do you have a safety pin?" I asked.

She fished around the kitchen while we exchanged knowing smiles. When she returned with the pin, I immediately grabbed it and pricked my thumb. The small jolt of pain was well worth it—when she saw my silver blood, Dr. Mason was instantly paralyzed with shock.

"Am I responsible for that?" she asked, staring at the silver dot on my thumb.

"We were going to ask you the same question," I replied.

"Looks like I've got some explaining to do," Dr. Mason said. She poured another round of tea and pulled up a chair.

"This all started," she began, "in my first job after graduate school. I had just gotten my Ph.D., and I was working for a big pharmaceutical company in Chicago. They wanted me to continue research on a paper I'd written for my degree, on how human genes might be combined with genes of different animals to create new, better supergenes. The drug company thought that my work might be a way to make humans resistant to disease. But until we could actually prove something in a laboratory, it was all science fiction."

Dr. Mason got a dreamy, far-off look in her eyes. "And it remained science fiction for seven long years. Failure after failure. I just couldn't quite attach the animal genes to the human genes. Finally the company ran out of money to waste on my project. They offered me a position on another experiment, but I turned them down. This was my life's work."

She smiled at us. "As it turned out, getting fired was the best thing that ever happened to me. I'd decided to come back to Metier, my hometown, where my dad was still living. I had packed all my things and was ready to go. And then the strangest thing happened."

She plunked the rock down in the center of the table. "My father, Professor Reginald Mason, is a geologist. He'd given me this meteor fragment on my eighteenth birthday as a good luck token. But I'd totally forgotten about it until I was packing up to leave Chicago. There it was, at the bottom of my sock drawer. That night I performed one final experiment, this time with Dad's good luck rock on my desk. Silly, right?"

None of us answered. We were all staring at the strange, metallic rock.

"But do you know what?" She looked around at our expectant faces. "It worked! Success! Somehow— I'm still not sure how—the rock affected the DNA, because after eleven years of failure, my theory had triumphed. I had never been so happy in my life. And on the plane back to Metier it hit me: Why limit my experiments to helping people stop catching colds? There were all sorts of other directions to be tried! You could let someone breathe underwater, or give them superhuman reflexes, or . . ." Her voice trailed off. "Well, the applications seemed limitless.

"Being happy about your work is one thing," she continued. "But I was careless. The minute I landed in Metier, I called all my friends to tell them about my results. I wrote my book, even posted some of my basic data on the Internet. I set up a lab right here in Metier, the one you saw next door, and started verifying my results. Sure enough, I was right. I was on to something big. And big people started to notice."

"So, do you know who ransacked your lab, then?" Toni asked.

"Well, for the past couple of weeks I've been getting calls from someone at the Pentagon who is interested in hiring me for my research. Once I realized he was in the Department of Defense, I told him that I wasn't interested in helping to create weapons. I'm afraid we didn't have a very pleasant conversation. The gentleman concluded by telling

117

me that he'd get my experiments one way or another. Then he hung up."

"That makes sense," Elena said. "We know that it's the government that makes the Omegas."

"But what doesn't make sense . . . ," Dr. Mason said, squinting, "is that they took all my lab equipment and notebooks but left the most important ingredient—the lucky rock."

"There's only one answer," I replied quickly. "They would leave it behind only if they already had more of the metal it was made from."

"But that's impossible," she retorted. "There aren't anymore rocks like this. It fell from space!"

I remembered the black trucks that had almost run us over. The same ones we saw again by the reservoir. I remembered the men we'd seen loading something heavy into the back of one of those trucks. Suddenly I had a pretty good idea what that something was.

"Actually, ma'am, I think your dad's rock is just a little fragment from a larger meteorite. One that crashed here millions of years ago."

"Are you talking about the meteor that created the reservoir?" Elena asked.

I nodded.

"Why won't that place *go away?*" Toni wailed. "Every time we turn around, there it is again. It's like, *following* us!"

"But Todd," Elena said, with a questioning look

118

on her face, "when Mr. Holland taught us about meteors in science class, he said that the impact was like a bomb going off. The crater out at Metier reservoir is a half mile wide. Wouldn't the meteor have been destroyed on impact?"

"If it was a normal meteor, maybe," I replied, "but I have a feeling there's something else about this rock, something we don't know. In any case, I'd bet anything that when we spied on those black trucks by the reservoir, we were watching a meteor removal in progress."

"Then we've lost," Dr. Mason said. "That's all the government needs to build the Omegas. There's no way to stop them."

"Well, then," Toni said thoughtfully, "why don't we steal it from them?"

"Steal it from them?" I asked. "They undoubtedly have it under tight security, and the Pentagon takes security pretty seriously."

"Besides which," Dr. Mason added, "that meteor could be in any one of a dozen government laboratories in a dozen states across the country."

"It is *now*," Toni answered, "but it wasn't yesterday."

"What are you suggesting?" Dr. Mason asked. "That we travel *backward* in *time?*"

The three of us kids shared a look.

"We should probably travel back before the impact crater became a reservoir," Elena mused, "before it

119

filled with water. Otherwise the meteor will be difficult to get to."

"Fascinating," Dr. Mason said. "You can actually travel into the past?"

"Yes," I told her. "That's the good part."

Suddenly the air was filled with a loud humming. Our teacups rattled in their saucers. A harsh light bathed the windows of the small cottage. "If we don't get out of here in a hurry," Toni squawked, "I think we're about to see the *bad* part!"

I slowly parted the curtain, being careful not to show myself through the window.

The Omega ship was hanging over the little house. There was no way out—not on foot, anyway. "It's the Omegas! They've found us!"

"We've got to jump," Elena said, "now!"

"Wait a second, guys," Toni protested, "I need some time to prepare! If we just jump that far back, with no warning, it'll make a timequake for sure!"

"That's the risk we have to take," I replied. "Our lives depend on it."

I could hear the beams of the house creaking under the force of the Omega ship. The floorboards were shuddering. It sounded as if they were trying to rip it off its foundations! "Come on, Toni!" Elena screamed. "We've got to get out of here!"

"Mom," Toni said, looking at the ceiling, "when I made that promise, I probably should have warned you . . . my life *is* one long emergency!"

"Go on. I'll hide in the tornado cellar," Dr. Mason told us. "They're not after me, anyway. Save yourselves!"

We linked hands. Toni closed her eyes, concentrating. The whole house was now swaying from side to side. I prayed silently that she was able to work up the energy she needed under the circumstances.

"Good luck," Dr. Mason called out to us.

Then there was an intense burst of light, and we were gone.

_____Chapter 16

Jack

If you have to travel anywhere, I can highly recommend not using an Omegan time ship. Particularly if you are a prisoner at the time. It's the pits. I'm talking *The Guinness Book of World Records*' "Worst Way to Travel," hands down.

Maybe you don't believe me. Maybe you once had to drive somewhere with your friend and your friend's kid brother, and you were all crunched up in the backseat for hours, and then the kid brother threw up all over himself, and maybe you think *that's* the worst. But it isn't. Not by a long shot. Trust me on this.

Or if you want, don't trust me, and try being suspended in a vat of yellow slop for ten hours at the rear end of a spacecraft that wasn't built with humans in mind. *That's* suffering. Until you've tried that, everything else is like a night on a down mattress.

To make matters worse, all of a sudden our captors' ship started shaking like a washing machine having a nervous breakdown. I was starting to feel a little sick.

What if I had to hurl? Barf? Upchuck? Yack? Food sneeze? Try the egg toss? Do the Technicolor yawn? I had about ten more ways to say vomit, but the more I thought about the subject, the more it was likely to happen. And the image of my lunch, suspended directly in front of me for the next month, was more than I could handle.

As if some higher power heard me, the ship began lurching violently from side to side. Not good. I was now desperately trying to hold on to the contents of my stomach.

The shaking got even worse. I could see the Omegas getting thrown about in the main cabin, frantically trying to hold on to the side rails. I would have laughed if I wasn't so close to puking.

That was when I realized: Something was really wrong. The ship was totally out of control. And then I figured it out.

Timequake!

The prison tubes rocked wildly back and forth. As the yellow goop sloshed around me I braced myself for the worst: I was about to become the first person ever to drown in a spaceship.

With a *snap!* the tube broke free of its base and toppled onto its side. *Great*, I thought. Not only was I a prisoner on an alien spacecraft, I was now also rolling around. Perhaps I'd end up as a nifty toy for some little Omegas: *Hey, kids! It's Jack-in-the-Can: The Screaming Boy That Rolls!*

Thud! My tube hit something, and I turned around to see Ethan's blurred face. He was pressed up against the glass of his fallen goop tube, trying to get my attention. He pointed toward the main control room, where several Omegas were scrambling toward the rear door. The sign above the door said Escape Pod. Not all that comforting.

I looked back at Ethan, who had rolled over toward an instrument panel at the back of the room. His face, barely visible through the mass of yellow slime, was clearly panicked. I soon realized why—a huge monitor on the panel was flashing *Emergency* with a little timer underneath counting down the seconds.

23 . . . 22 . . . 21 . . . 20 . . .

It suddenly occurred to me: *Either these Omegas throw one crazy New Year's party, or I have twenty seconds to live. . . .*

———— Chapter 17

Toni

"What do you want me to say?" I squeaked miserably. "You said to go far back."

"Well," Todd said bitterly, "this is *certainly* far enough."

We were looking at the vast, rock-strewn plain where the Metier reservoir would someday be built. That's right: the vast *plain*. No forest. No crater. The meteor hadn't even hit yet.

"Look," I snarled, "I've been through a lot today. I'm wearing a dumb T-shirt. A bunch of stupid hicks called me names. My dead mother told me I'm not good at following directions. I was arrested for a felony, and then the arresting officers turned out to be Omegas, and then the Omegas tried to run me over with a police cruiser. All right? This is not how I expected to spend my teenage years. So next time you want someone to jump you millions of years into the past with pinpoint accuracy, why don't you do it yourself?"

"You don't have to get defensive," Todd returned.

"I'm just saying, it would probably be easier to swipe the meteor if it were actually here, *on Earth*, and not still out there, in *deep space*. Okay? It's not your fault. It's no one's fault. It's—"

"—*coming*," Elena said, cutting him off.

"What?" Todd and I asked at the same time.

Elena was swaying slightly from side to side. Her eyelids fluttered. She was in a powerful trance, no doubt about it. "It's coming," Elena repeated. "The meteor. It's headed directly for us."

"When?" Todd asked. "In a month? A year?"

"Now," Elena answered, her eyes snapping wide. "Any *minute* now! We have to run!"

Instinctively we all looked up at the skies. Sure enough, the clouds were lit up with a fierce light that was plummeting toward us. "Too late," Todd muttered.

I suddenly realized we were about to die. "Elena," I said, putting a comforting hand on her shoulder, "if I've ever said anything that hurt your feelings, about your hair or anything, I want you to know that I'm—"

She wasn't listening to me. "Hey," she exclaimed. "That's not a meteor! That's—"

Her words were drowned out as the streak touched down fifty or so yards from us. To our surprise and relief, it sounded more like a bad car crash than an apocalyptic collision. Whatever created the Metier crater, this wasn't it.

"It's the Omega ship!" Elena finished. "We must have dragged it through time with us!"

"You don't suppose Ethan and the others were on board?" Todd asked, his voice weak.

I sure hope not, I thought.

We rushed over to the spot where the craft had crash-landed. Metal was scattered all over the plains. It looked like the photographs of airplane wrecks I'd seen in magazines. A plume of inky black smoke rose from the crash site. We didn't dare touch the ship: It was still white-hot from reentry. Scorch marks pocked its sides, and the air was filled with the acrid smell of burning metal.

"I'm sure those guys made it off the—," I wished out loud.

"What is *that?*"

A yellow cylinder—like an overgrown test tube—rolled out from under the chronosphere and halted about twenty feet to our left. I walked over to inspect it but stopped short when it started rocking back and forth. And if that wasn't eerie enough, the test tube seemed to be calling—more like whispering—my name.

"Tooonniiii!"

It sounded like Jack. Could he have possibly survived that crash? I took another step and saw Jack's slimy face pressed against the side of the tube. Of course! It was an Omega holding tank.

127

I pushed my hand toward Jack's face, and it left an imprint in the soft, waxy plastic shell of the tube.

"*Tooonniiii! I'm not a museum exhibit! Let me out of here!*"

We cut the tube open with Todd's pocketknife, and Jack emerged like a baby from the womb. He wiped his face and blinked, trying to get rid of the goo.

"Are you all right?" I asked.

"Yeah, great. Really relaxed. In fact, I think I'm going to get me a tube of that yellow stuff for back home, and every so often I'll dunk myself in it. You know, for kicks," Jack replied.

A voice came from behind us. "Joke all you want, Jack, but that yellow goop saved our lives!"

We turned around. There, looking like she had been through Jell-O Armageddon, was Ashley. She limped toward us. Silver blood trickled from a small cut on her forehead, but other than that she looked fine.

"Don't ask, because I don't know what happened. When I regained consciousness, I was lying on the ground in a pile of goop. By the way, where *are* we?" Ashley stammered.

"We're in Metier, and we're waiting for the—"

Midsentence, I noticed that Todd and Elena were staring into the sky behind me, mouths agape.

"Turn around, Toni," Elena said, not taking her eyes off the sky.

From her tone of voice, I knew I wasn't being asked to look at a pretty rainbow or a cloud that was shaped like a bunny rabbit. No, this was something bad.

I was unprepared for just *how* bad.

There, in a fiery blaze of glory, was the *real* meteor, the one that would create the reservoir, and the Omega experiments, and us. We weren't directly in its path, but I had read about the destructive aftermath of meteor collisions. Our only hope was to run from the shockwaves.

"Before we sprint out of here . . . where is Ethan?" I asked.

"He's not with you? Then he must be—" Ashley looked with dread toward the smoking ship.

"You guys make a run for it," I told them. "I have to find Ethan." Ashley started to protest, but I held up my hand. "Don't argue with me. You got to be the hero last time. It's my turn now."

"But Toni," Todd said, "what about you? Even if you free him, you won't have enough time to get away."

"Maybe not," I answered. "But *someone* has to get Ethan out of that mound of scrap metal. Someone who has an arc welder for an arm. And I'm the only person who fits that description."

"Toni, you can't do it," Jack stated. "That's that."

"Wrong," I replied, "I can do it. Although it's sweet of you to try to stop me. And I'll tell you something else. My life isn't in any danger. I've got a plan."

They just looked at me. I knew that any one of them would have taken my place. But I felt like I was the only one who could do this job.

"Please," I said. "Get out of here. Before it's too late for all of us." Without giving them another chance to object, I turned and crawled into the ship.

If it weren't for the moaning, I never would have found him.

Guided by Ethan's panicked voice, I made my way through smashed machinery and crumpled corridors. He was out of his holding tank—what remained of it lay in the corner, dripping goo. Ethan was in the opposite corner, trapped under a huge instrument control panel. An immense metal box had ripped loose from the wall, pinning his leg. "Are you all right?" I asked.

Okay. I know. *Dumb question.*

"It's not broken or anything. I just can't seem to get loose." Ethan tugged on his leg with all his might. Even with his superstrength, he was getting nowhere. The only way that he was going to get out of there was if someone cut through the metal that held his limb in place. And that someone was me.

"Don't worry," I told him. "I'll get you out of there."

I placed my hands palms down on the giant

computer. Luckily I could still detect an electric current pulsing inside. I concentrated and suddenly could feel the energy flowing into me, like soda through a straw. I hoped there was enough. I'd need every volt I could muster.

"So," I said, casually trying to change the subject as I charged myself, "where did all the Omegas go?" I looked around the wrecked cabin. There was no sign of our bug-eyed enemies.

"They locked themselves into the escape pod," Ethan said, and almost laughed. "I bet they're sorry now."

"Why's that?" I asked.

"Because *that's* the escape pod," he replied, nodding toward a solid mass of mangled metal at the very bottom of the wreckage. "Not much of an escape, would you say?"

I started to nod, and that's when I heard it.

It was sort of like thunder, sort of like a flag being whipped in a violent wind.

The meteor. Entering Earth's atmosphere. Burning up the sky. Getting closer.

I removed my hands from the computer.

Looks like this is as charged as I'm going to get.

When Ethan spoke again, his voice was small and scared. "Are we really gonna make it, Toni?"

I looked him straight in the eye. "There isn't a doubt in my mind. Now hold still," I warned him as electricity coursed through my fingertips like a laser. "This may sting a bit."

_____ Chapter 18

Ashley

The four of us raced toward the horizon, neck and neck, our legs pounding the odd, spongy ground as fast as we could will them. There was no cover, no big boulders, not even a tree to hide behind. Just the rolling hills and the cool evening air, neither of which would do much to protect us from the blast of an incoming meteor.

Just as we began to slow down and pant heavily, we hit the end of the line.

I looked down; we were at the top of a steep, near-vertical drop. At the bottom of the cliff, about fifty feet below, was a crystal-clear lake.

"Tell me we're *not* going to do what I think we're about to do," Elena said weakly as Jack took her hand in his own. He held out his free hand to me. I grabbed it with my left hand and Todd's with my right. We squeezed tight.

Then just like that, we jumped—screaming, falling—

Ploosh! Ploosh! Ploosh!

—and hit the water.

"We should be safe here!" Todd shouted while treading water beside me. I looked at his bobbing head and was shocked to see that his skin had turned green. I thought he might be ill until I realized that the entire sky was lit with an eerie, greenish white light as the meteor punched through the upper atmosphere like a giant flaming fist. A sonic boom forced me back underwater, followed by a warbling scream like that of a soaring bottle rocket before it explodes—only a million times louder.

"I hope Toni and Ethan get out in time!" Elena shouted at me. She was probably yelling at the top of her lungs, but I still had to read her lips to understand.

"Me too!" I gurgled back.

But I had my doubts. A couple of times, as we were running, I'd peered back over my shoulder, hoping to see Toni and Ethan running after us—or maybe the telltale flash that signified a successful time jump. But I hadn't seen anything.

I said a silent prayer for my two friends and then, looking up at the flickering green sky, I said a prayer for myself.

The sound of impact was deafening—like two rifles being fired right next to my ears. Then there was a second of eerie safety before the shock wave hit, which tossed me about twenty feet in the air. I was bombarded with pebbles and dust, then plunged back underwater. After a moment's refuge the water shot me back into the air like an insane washing machine. Plunge.

133

Shoot. Plunge. Shoot. It was actually kind of fun.

Amidst this chaos, I found myself right next to Elena in midair. Her face was pale and she was coughing heavily. *Of course, you idiot,* I thought, *not everyone has the power to breathe underwater . . .*

With little time to plan, I entered the water and dove deep, fighting against the turbulence. I swam deep enough that the tides merely jostled me around like a feisty wind. *I'll just sit here and save my energy . . .*

Soon, the water calmed and my mission was on. I shot upward, looking for legs. I finally found a pair, grabbed for the waistline, and started swimming toward the distant shore. I felt an elbow jab my ribs, and looked over at Todd's terrified face.

"I'm trying to help, Todd!" I said, a little peeved.

He just gurgled and coughed, but his changed expression showed his relief.

I swam Todd to the shore, coughing the whole way. After setting him down on the sand facedown, I took off his shirt and threw it over his head to keep the dusty air out of his lungs. Pausing for a moment to regain strength, I looked around. The air was so thick with dust that the sun was barely visible. As far as I could see, the world was a hazy, swirling cloud of gray, and the earth still trembled beneath me.

"Assshhh—"

In the dirty distance, Elena's pale face gasped, and then went under. I was instantly in the water, moving toward the spot where I had seen her. No

Elena, anywhere. Diving deep, I saw her limp body drift helplessly downward like a leaf falling from a tree. I lugged her body slowly, slowly toward the shore. Arms aching, heart pounding, I reached the shore . . . and collapsed.

"Come on, Ashley. Come on—"

Someone was tugging at my shirt and slapping my cheeks lightly.

"I'm not gonna have to save Aquagirl, too, am I?" Jack's sarcasm couldn't cover up traces of panic in his voice.

"You sure aren't, Superboy," I replied with a weak smile. "Where's Elena?" I asked, suddenly remembering my nearly drowned friend.

"Right here, Ash. You saved my life," Elena answered.

"With a little help from the doctor!" Jack chimed in.

"Yeah, Jack claims he swam to shore, saw me coughing up water, and gave me mouth-to-mouth resuscitation, but I'm not buying his hero's tale," Elena said. I couldn't tell whether she was joking or not.

I gathered the strength to sit upright. The dust had settled a bit, but it was still hard to breathe.

"Let's get to the matter at hand. How far back are we?" Todd wondered. "A thousand years? Twenty thousand?"

"More like a million," Jack put in. "This is long before man first showed his face. Anything could be out here."

"How are we going to get home?" I asked. "What can we do?"

"There's only one thing we *can* do," Todd replied. "Wait for Toni. Hope she remembers to come back and save us."

"Hope she *survived*," I added, staring into the crater's depths.

Either Toni had freed Ethan in time and they'd time-jumped to safety . . . or we were about to spend our final days in a prehistoric wasteland.

I shivered.

The sun was a scarlet disk on the horizon. It was going to be dark soon. And cold. I gathered my wet T-shirt about me, suddenly realizing how inadequately I was dressed. How all of us were dressed.

In the distance there came a sound—an animal sound—long and lonely, like the song of a whale or the howl of a wolf.

One thing was certain: Whatever was making it, it wasn't alone.

It was soon answered by another howl. And another. Then more.

For the first time in a long time, the Omegas seemed to be the least of our worries.

About the Author

Chris Archer grew up in New Jersey, where he spent most of his childhood wishing he had special powers.

He now divides his time between New York City and Los Angeles, California. When Chris is not writing books and screenplays, he enjoys going to scary movies, playing piano (badly), and reading suspense novels.

He has never been to Wisconsin.

Don't miss

mindwarp

Meltdown

Coming in mid-January
From MINSTREL Paperbacks